J. T. Trowbridge

The young surveyor

J. T. Trowbridge

The young surveyor

ISBN/EAN: 9783744680950

Printed in Europe, USA, Canada, Australia, Japan

Cover: Foto ©Andreas Hilbeck / pixelio.de

More available books at **www.hansebooks.com**

THE

YOUNG SURVEYOR;

OR,

JACK ON THE PRAIRIES.

BY

J. T. TROWBRIDGE,

AUTHOR OF "JACK HAZARD AND HIS FORTUNES," ETC.

WITH ILLUSTRATIONS.

BOSTON:

JAMES R. OSGOOD AND COMPANY,

LATE TICKNOR & FIELDS, AND FIELDS, OSGOOD, & CO.

1875.

University Press : Welch, Bigelow, & Co.,
Cambridge.

CONTENTS.

CHAPTER   PAGE

I. "Nothing but a Boy" 7

II. Old Wiggett's Section Corner . . 16

III. The Homeward Track 25

IV. A Deer Hunt, and how it ended . . 32

V. The Boy with One Suspender . . . 41

VI. "Lord Betterson's" 47

VII. Jack at the "Castle" 53

VIII. How Vinnie made a Journey . . 62

IX. Vinnie's Adventure 68

X. Jack and Vinnie in Chicago . . . 75

XI. Jack's New Home 82

XII. Vinnie's Future Home 92

XIII. Why Jack did not fire at the Prairie Chicken 97

XIV. Snowfoot's New Owner 104

XV. Going for a Witness 115

XVI. Peakslow gets a Quirk in his Head . 120

XVII. Vinnie makes a Beginning . . . 126

XVIII. Vinnie's new Broom 133

XIX. Link's Wood-Pile 140

XX. More Water than they wanted . 148

XXI. Peakslow shows his Hand . . . 157

XXII. The Woodland Spring . . . 161

XXIII. Jack's "Bit of Engineering" . . 167

XXIV. Preparing for the Attack . . 178

XXV. The Battle of the Boundary Fence . 184

XXVI. Victory 189

XXVII. Vinnie in the Lion's Den . . . 196

XXVIII. An "Extraordinary" Girl . . 204

XXIX. Another Hunt, and how it ended . 211

XXX. Jack's Prisoner 219

XXXI. Radcliff 222

XXXII. An Important Event 231

XXXIII. Mrs. Wiggett's "Noon-Mark" . . 235

XXXIV. The Strange Cloud 242

XXXV. Peakslow in a Tight Place. — Cecie . 249

XXXVI. "On the War Trail" . . . 263

XXXVII. The Mystery of a Pair of Breeches. 268

XXXVIII. The Morning after 272

XXXIX. Following up the Mystery . . . 276

XL. Peakslow's House-Raising . . 280

XLI. Conclusion 287

LIST OF ILLUSTRATIONS.

	PAGE
SETTING THE STAKES .	17
JACK AND THE STRANGE YOUTH .	36
UP-HILL WORK .	45
"LORD BETTERSON" .	49
TOO OBLIGING BY HALF .	71
LINK DOES N'T CARE TO BE KISSED	93
SHOT ON THE WING .	102
THE AMIABLE MR. PEAKSLOW .	107
VINNIE'S STRATAGEM .	129
LINK'S WOOD-PILE .	144
HOW THE BOYS WENT TO THE RIVER FOR WATER .	154
TESTING THE LEVEL .	168
OLD WIGGETT .	178
"STOP, OR I'LL SHOOT!" .	187
RETURNING IN TRIUMPH .	195
THE END OF THE CHASE .	216
JACK AND HIS JOLLY PRISONER .	222
THE TORNADO COMING .	248
PEAKSLOW REAPPEARS .	256
FOLLOWING THE WAR TRAIL UNDER DIFFICULTIES .	268
THE WATER QUESTION SETTLED .	288

THE YOUNG SURVEYOR.

CHAPTER I.

"NOTHING BUT A BOY."

YOUNG fellow in a light buggy, with a big black dog sitting composedly beside him, enjoying the ride, drove up, one summer afternoon, to the door of a log-house, in one of the early settlements of Northern Illinois.

A woman with lank features, in a soiled gown trailing its rags about her bare feet, came and stood in the doorway and stared at him.

"Does Mr. Wiggett live here?" he inquired.

"Wal, I reckon," said the woman, "'f he ain't dead or skedaddled of a sudden."

"Is he at home?"

"Wal, I reckon."

"Can I see him?"

"I dunno noth'n' to hender. Yer, Sal! run up in the burnt lot and fetch your pap. Tell him a stranger. You've druv a good piece," the woman added, glancing at the buggy-wheels and the horse's white feet, stained with black prairie soil.

"I've driven over from North Mills," replied the young fellow, regarding her pleasantly, with bright, honest features, from under the shade of his hat-brim.

"I 'lowed as much. Alight and come into the house. Old man'll be yer in a minute."

He declined the invitation to enter; but, to rest his limbs, leaped down from the buggy. Thereupon the dog rose from his seat on the wagon-bottom, jumped down after him, and shook himself.

"All creation!" said the woman, "what a pup that ar is! Yer, you young uns! Put back into the house, and hide under the bed, or he'll eat ye up like ye was so much cl'ar soap-grease!"

At that moment the dog stretched his great mouth open, with a formidable yawn. Panic seized the "young uns," and they scampered; their bare legs and exceedingly scanty attire (only three shirts and a half to four little barbarians) seeming to offer the dog unusual facilities, had he chosen to regard them as soap-grease and to regale himself on that sort of diet. But he was too well-bred and good-natured an

animal to think of snapping up a little Wiggett or
two for his luncheon ; and the fugitives, having first
run under the bed and looked out, ventured back to
the door, and peeped with scared faces from behind
their mother's gown.

To hide his laughter, the young fellow stood pat-
ting and stroking his horse's neck until Sal returned
with her " pap."

" Mr. Wiggett ? " inquired the youth, seeing a tall,
spare, rough old man approach.   · ·

" That's my name, stranger.   What can I dew for
ye to-day ? "

" I 've come to see what I can do for *you*, Mr.
Wiggett.   I believe you want your section corner
looked up."

" That I dew, stranger.   But I 'lowed 't would take
a land-surveyor for that."

" I am a land-surveyor," said the young fellow,
with a modest smile.

" A land-surveyor ?   Why, you 're noth'n' but a
boy !"   And the tall old man, bending a little, and
knitting his gray eyebrows, looked down upon his
visitor with a sort of amused curiosity.

" That's so," replied the " boy," with a laugh and a
blush.   " But I think I can find your corner, if the
bearings are all right."

" Whur's your instruments ? " asked the old man,
leaning over the buggy.   " Them all ?   What's that
gun to do with land-surveyin' ? "

" Nothing ; I brought that along, thinking I might
1 *

get a shot at a rabbit or a prairie hen. But we shall need an axe and a shovel."

" I 'lowed your boss would come himself, in place of sendin' a boy !" muttered the old man, taking up the gun, — a light double-barrelled fowling-piece, — sighting across it with an experienced eye, and laying it down again. " Sal, bring the axe ; it 's stickin' in the log thar by the wood-pile. Curi's thing, to lose my section corner, hey ?"

" It 's not a very uncommon thing," replied the young surveyor.

" Fact is," said the old man, " I never found it. I bought of Seth Parkins's widder arter Seth died, and banged if I 've ever been able to find the gov'ment stake."

" Maybe somebody pulled it up, or broke it off, to kill a rattlesnake with," suggested the young surveyor.

" Like enough," said the old man. " Can't say 't I blame him ; though he might 'a' got a stick in the timber by walkin' a few rods. He could n't 'a' been so bad off as one o' you surveyor chaps was when the gov'ment survey went through. He was off on the Big Perairie, footin' it to his camp, when he comes to a rattler curled up in the grass, and shakin' his tarnal buzz-tail at him. He steps back, and casts about him for some sort of we'pon ; he had n't a thing in his fist but a roll of paper, and if ever a chap hankered arter a stick or a stun, they say he did. But it was all jest perairie grass ; nary rock nor a piece of timber within three mile. Snake seemed to 'preciate his advantage, and flattened his head and whirred his rattle sassier 'n ever. Surveyor chap could n't stan' that. So what does he dew, like a blamed fool, but jest off with his boot and hurl it, 'lowin' he could kill a rattler that way? He missed shot. Then, to git his boot, he had to pull off t' other, and tackle the snake with that. Lost that tew. Then he was in a perdickerment; snake got both boots; curled up on tew 'em, ready to strike, and seemin' to say, ' If you 've any more boots to spar', bring 'em on.' Surveyor chap had n't no more boots, to his sorrow; and, arter layin' siege to the critter till sundown, hopin' he 'd depart in peace and leave him his property, he guv it up as a bad job, and footed it to the camp in his stockin's, fancyin' he was treadin' among rattlers all the way."

The story was finished by the time the axe was brought; the old man picked up a rusty shovel lying by the house, and, getting into the buggy with his tools, he pointed out to his young companion a rough road leading through the timber.

This was a broad belt of woodland, skirting the eastern side of a wide, fertile river-bottom, and giving to the settlement the popular name of " Long Woods."

On the other side of the timber lay the high prairie region, covered with coarse wild grass, and spotted with flowers, without tree or shrub visible until another line of timber, miles away, marked the vicinity of another stream.

The young surveyor and the old man, in the jolting buggy, followed by the dog, left the log-house and the valley behind them; traversed the woods, through flickering sun and shade; and drove southward along the edge of the rolling prairie, until the old man said they had better stop and hitch.

" I don't hitch my horse," said the young surveyor. "The dog looks out for him. Here, old fellow, watch !"

" The section corner, I ca'c'late," said the old man, shouldering his axe, " is off on the perairie thar, some'er's. Come, and I 'll show ye the trees."

" Is that big oak with the broken limb one of them ? "

" Wal, now, how did ye come to guess that ? — one tree out of a hundred ye might 'a' picked."

" It is a prominent tree," replied the youth, " and, if I had been the surveyor, I think I should have chosen it for one, to put my bearings on."

" Boy, you 're right ! But it took me tew days to decide even that. The underbrush has growed up around it, and the old scar has nigh about healed over."

The old man led the way through the thickets, and, reaching a small clear space at the foot of the great oak, pointed out the scar, where the trunk had been blazed by the axemen of the government survey. On a surface about six inches broad, hewed for the purpose, the distance and direction of the tree from the corner stake had, no doubt, been duly marked. But only a curiously shaped wound was left. The growth of the wood was rapid in that rich region, and, although the cut had been made but a few years before, a broad lip of smooth new bark had rolled up about it from the sides, and so nearly closed over it that only a narrow, perpendicular, dark slit remained.

"What do you make of that?" said Mr. Wiggett, putting his fingers at the opening, and looking down at his companion.

"I don't make much of it as it looks now," the young surveyor replied.

"Didn't I tell you 'twould take an old head to find my corner? T' other tree is in a wus shape than this yer. Now I reckon you'll be satisfied to turn about and whip home, and tell your boss it's a job for him."

"Give me your axe," was the reply.

"Boy, take kere what you're about!"

"O, I will take care; don't be afraid!" And, grasping the axe, the young surveyor began to cut away the folds of new wood which had formed over the scar.

"I see what you're up tew," said the old man, gaining confidence at every stroke. "Give me the axe; you ain't tall enough to work handy." And with a few strokes, being a skilful chopper, he cleared the old blaze, and exposed the blackened tablet which Nature had so nearly enclosed in her casket of living wood.

There, cut into the old hewed surface, were the well-preserved marks of the government survey:

N. 48° 15′ W.

18 R. 10 L.

"What does that mean?" asked the old man, as the youth made a copy of these marks in his note-book.

"It means that this tree is eighteen rods and ten links from your corner stake, in a direction forty-eight degrees and fifteen minutes west of north."

"I can understand your rods and links," said the old man; "for I know your surveyor's chain is four rods long, and has a hundred links. But banged if I know anything about your degrees and minutes."

"All that is just as simple," replied the young surveyor. "A circle is supposed to be divided into three hundred and sixty degrees. Each degree is divided into sixty minutes; and so forth. Now, if you stand looking directly north, then turn a quarter of the way round, and look straight west, you have turned a quarter of a circle, or ninety degrees; and the angle where you stand — where the north line and the west line meet — is called an angle of ninety degrees. Half as far is forty-five degrees. Seen from the corner stake, wherever it is, this tree bears a little more than forty-five degrees west of north; it is forty-eight degrees and a quarter. Where's the other tree?"

That was ten or eleven rods away, still in the edge of the timber; and it bore on its blazed trunk, facing the open prairie, the inscription — laid bare by the old man's ready axe —

N. 82° 27′ w.
16 R. 29 L.

"Eighty-two degrees twenty-seven minutes west of north, and sixteen rods twenty-nine links, from your corner," the young surveyor read aloud, as he copied the marks into his note-book. "The other tree is so surrounded by undergrowth, it would take you and your axe an hour to cut a passage through so that I could run a line; and I am going to try running a line from this tree alone. Be cutting a few good stakes, while I go and bring up my horse and set him to eating grass."

CHAPTER II.

OLD WIGGETT'S SECTION CORNER.

THE horse was driven to a good shady place on the edge of the woods, relieved of his bridle, and left in charge of the dog. In the mean while the old man cut a few oak saplings and hewed them into stakes.

"Now, I want ye to give me a notion of how you're gwine to work," he said, as the youth brought his compass and set it up on its tripod at the foot of the tree. "For, otherwise, how am I to be sure of my corner, when you say you've found it?"

"O, I think we shall find something to convince you! However, look here, and I'll explain."

While waiting for the wavering needle to settle in its place, the youth made a hasty diagram in a page of his note-book.

"Here we are on the edge of the timber. *A* is your first tree. *B* is the one where we are. Now if the bearings are correct, and I run two lines accordingly, the place where they meet will be the place for your corner stake; say at *C*."

"That looks cute; I like the shape of that!" said the old man, interested.

"If the distance was short, — feet instead of rods,

SETTING THE STAKES. — Page 18.

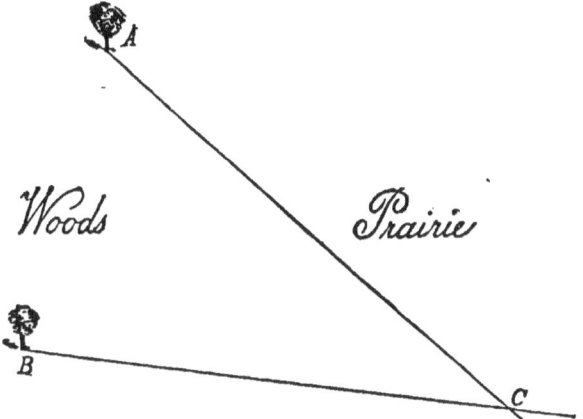

—all the instruments we should want," said the young surveyor, with his peculiarly bright smile, "would be a foot measure and two strings."

"How so?" said the old man, who could not believe that science was as simple a thing as that.

"Why, for instance, we will say the tree A is eighteen feet from the corner you want to find; B, sixteen feet. Now take a string eighteen feet long, and fasten the end of it by a nail to the centre of the blazed trunk, A; fasten another sixteen feet long to B; then stretch out the loose ends of both until they just meet; and there is the place for your stake."

"I declar'!" exclaimed the old man. "That's the use of the tew trees. Banged if I dew see, though, how you're gwine to git along by runnin' a line from jest one."

"If I run two lines, as I have shown you, where

B

they meet will be the point. Now if I run one line, and measure it, I shall find the point where the other line ought to meet it. We 'll see. Here on my compass is a circle and a scale of degrees, which shows me how to set it according to the bearings. Now look through these sights, and you are looking straight in the direction of your section corner."

"Curi's, ain't it ?" grinned the old man. "'Cordin' to that, my corner is out on the perairie, jest over beyant that ar knoll."

"You 're right. Now go forward to the top of it, while I sight you, and we 'll set a stake there. As I signal with my hands this way, or this, move your stake to the right or left, till I make *this* motion; then you are all right."

The young surveyor had got his compass into position, by looking back through the sights at the tree. He now placed himself between it and the tree, and, sighting forward, directed the old man, who went on over the knoll, where to set his stakes.

On the other side of the knoll, it was found that the line crossed a slough, — or "slew," as the old man termed it, — which lay in a long, winding hollow of the hills. This morass was partly filled with stagnant water; and the old man gave it a bad name.

"It 's the wust slew in the hull country. I 've lost tew cows in 't. I would n't go through it for the price of my farm. Could n't git through; a man would sink intew it up tew his neck."

"Then we may have to get a boat to find your section corner," laughed the young surveyor.

"But it's noth'n' but a bog this time o' year; ye can't navigate a boat thar. And it'll take till middle o' next week to build a brush road acrost. Guess we're up a stump now, hey?"

"O, no; stumps are not so plenty, where I undertake jobs! Let's have a stake down there, pretty near the *slew;* then we will measure our line, and see how much farther we have to go."

The old man helped bear the chain; and a careful measurement showed that the stake at the edge of the slough was still four rods and thirty links from the corner they sought.

"Banged if it don't come jest over on t' other side of the slew!" the old man exclaimed, computing the distance with his eye. "But we can't measure a rod furder; and yer we be stuck."

"Not yet, old friend!" cried the young surveyor. "Since we can't cross, we'll measure the rest of our distance along on this shore."

The old man looked down upon him with indignation and amazement.

"Think I'm a dog-goned fool?" he cried. "The idee of turnin' from our course, and measurin' along by the slew! What's the good of that?"

Finding that the old man would not aid or abet what seemed to him such complete folly, the young surveyor made another little diagram in his notebook, and explained: —

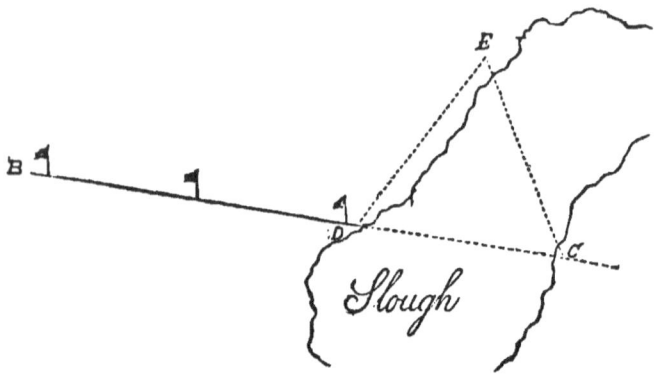

"Here is the end of our line running from the
direction B,—theoretically a straight, horizontal line,
though it curves over the knoll. You noticed how,
coming down the slope ahead of you, I held my end
of the chain up from the ground, to make it horizontal, and then with my plumb-line found the corre-
sponding point in the ground, to start fresh from.
That was to get the measurement of a horizontal
line; for if you measure all the ups and downs of
hills and hollows, you'll find your surveying will
come out in queer shape."

The old man scratched his bushy gray head, and
said he had n't thought of that.

"Well," the young surveyor continued, "we are
running our line off towards C, when we come to the
slew. Our last stake is at D,—say this little thing
with a flag on it. Now, what is to be done? for we
must measure four rods and thirty links farther. I
measure that distance from D to E, along this shore,
running my new line at an angle of sixty degrees

from the true course. Then, with my compass at E, I sight another line at an angle of sixty degrees from my last. I am making what is called an equilateral triangle; that is, a triangle with equal sides and equal angles. Each angle must measure sixty degrees. With two angles and one side, we can always get the other two sides; and the other angle will be where those two sides meet. They will meet at C. Now, since the sides are of equal length, the distance from D to C is the same as from D to E,— that is, four rods and thirty links, just the distance we wish to go; C, then, is the place for your corner stake."

"It looks very well on paper," said the old man, "but"—casting his eye across the bog—"how in the name of seven kingdoms are ye ever gwine to fix yer stake thar?"

"That is easy. Go round to the other side of the slew, get yourself in range with our line from the tree, by sighting across the stakes, and walk down toward the slew,— that is, on this dotted line. Having got my angle of sixty degrees at E, I will sight across and stop you when I see you at C. There stick your last stake."

"Banged if that ain't cute! Young man, what mout be your name?"

"I was only boy a few minutes ago," said the young surveyor, slyly. "Now, if you are ready, we'll set to work and carry out this plan."

The line from D to E was measured off. Then the youth set his compass to obtain the proper angle at

E; while the old man, with his axe and a fresh stake, tramped around to the eastern side of the slough. Having got the range of the stakes, he was moving slowly back toward them, holding his stake before him, when the youth signalled him to stop just in the edge of the quagmire.

The new stake stuck, the young surveyor, taking up his tripod and compass, went round to him.

" That stake," said he, " is not far from your corner. Are there any signs ? "

" I 've been thinkin'," said the old man, " the 'arth yer looks like it had been disturbed some time; though it 's all overgrowed so with these clumps of slew-grass, ye can't tell what 's a nat'ral hummock and what ain't. Don't that look like a kind of a trench ? "

" Yes ; and here 's another at right angles with it. Surveyors cut such places on the prairies, pile up the sods inside the angle, and drive their corner stakes through them. But there must have been water here when this job was done, which accounts for its not being done better. We 'll improve it. Go for the shovel. I 'll get the bearings of those trees in the mean while, and see how far wrong they make us out to be."

When the old man returned with the shovel, he found his boy surveyor standing by the compass, with folded arms, looking over at the woodland with a smile of satisfaction.

Sighting the trees, the tall, straight stems of which

.were both visible over the knoll, he had found that their bearings corresponded with those copied in his note-book. This proved his work to his own mind ; but the old man would not yet confess himself convinced.

"We may be somewhur *nigh* the spot, but I want to be sure of the *exact* spot,'' he insisted.

"That you can't be sure of; not even if the best surveyor in the world should come and get it from these bearings," replied the youth. "Probably the bearings themselves are not exact. The government surveyors do their work in a hurry. The common compass they use does n't make as fine angles as the theodolite or transit instrument does ; and then the chain varies a trifle in length with every variation of temperature ; the metal contracts and expands, you know. Surveying, where the land is worth a dollar and a quarter a foot, instead of a dollar and a quarter an acre, is done more carefully. Yet I am positive, from the indications here, that we are within a few inches of your corner."

" A few inches, or a few feet, or a few rods !" muttered the old man, crossly. " Seems like thar's a good deal of guess-work, arter all."

" I am sorry you think so," replied the young surveyor, quietly removing his tripod. " If, however, you are dissatisfied with my work, you can employ another surveyor; if he tells you I am far out of the way, why, then, you need n't pay me."

The old man made no reply, but, seizing the shovel,

began to level the hummock a little, in order to prepare it for a pile of fresh sods. He was slashing
away at it, with the air of a petulant man working off his discontent, when he struck something
hard.

" What's that ar ? " he growled. " Can't be a
stone. Ain't a rock as big as a hazel-nut this side
the timber."

Digging round the obstacle, he soon exposed the
splintered end of an upright piece of wood. He laid
hold of it and tried to pull it up. The youth, with
lively interest, took the shovel, and dug and pried.
Suddenly up came the stick, and the old man went
over backwards with it into the bog.

He scrambled to his feet, dripping with muddy
water, and brandished his trophy, exclaiming : —

" Dog my cats ! if 't ain't the eend of the ol' corner stake, left jest whur 't was broke off, when the
rest was wanted to pry a wheel out o' the slew, or to
kill a rattler with ! "

He appeared jubilant over the discovery, while the
young surveyor regarded it simply as a piece of good
luck.

CHAPTER III.

THE HOMEWARD TRACK.

THE new stake having been stuck in the hole left by the point of the old one, and plenty of fresh turf piled up about it, the old man wiped his fingers on the dry prairie-grass, thrust a hand into his pocket, and brought forth an ancient leather wallet.

"My friend," said he, "shall I settle with you or with your boss?"

"You may as well settle with me."

"Nuff said. What's yer tax?"

"Two dollars and a half."

"Tew dollars and a — dog-gone-ation! You've been only tew hours and a half about the job. I can hire a man all day for half a dollar."

"It is an afternoon's work for me," argued the young surveyor. "I've had a long way to drive. Then, you must understand, we surveyors" (this was said with an air of importance) "don't get pay merely for the time we are employed, but also for our knowledge of the business, which it has taken us time to learn. If I had been obliged to hire the horse I drive, you see, I should n't have much left out of two dollars and a half."

"Friend, you're right. Tew 'n' a half is reason-

2

able. And if I have another job of land-surveyin',
you are the man for my money."

"A man, am I, now?" And with a laugh the
young surveyor pocketed his fee.

"Good as a man, I allow, any time o' day. You've
worked at this yer thing right smart, and I'll give ye
the credit on 't. How long have ye been larnin the
trade?"

"O, two years, more or less, studying at odd spells!
But I never made a business of it until I came to
this new country."

"What State be ye from?"

"New York."

"York State! That 's whur I hail from."

"One would n't think so; you have a good many
Southern and Western words in your talk."

"I come by 'em honest," said the old man. "I
run away from home when I was a boy, like a derned
fool; I 've lived a'most everywhur; and I 've married
four wives, and raised four craps of children. My
fust wife I picked up in ol' Kaintuck. My next was
an Arkansaw woman. My third was a Michigander.
My present was born and raised in the South, but I
married her in Southern Illinois. She 's nigh on to
forty year younger 'n I be, and smart as a steel
trap, tell you! So you see we 're kind of a mixed-
up family. My fust and second broods of children 's married off, or buried, — scattered to the
four winds o' heaven! Tew boys o' the third brood,
and that ar Sal, is with me yit. Some of the pres-

ent brood you've seen. Thar's been twenty-one in all."

" Of the fourth brood ? " '

" No, of the lot. Whose hoss mout that be ? "

" Mine; I brought him from the East with me."

" What do you have to pay for a beast like that, now, in York State ? "

" I did n't pay anything for him."

" Somebody gi'n him tew ye ? "

" Not exactly."

" Ye gambled for him ? "

" No."

" Raised him from a colt, then ? "

" No."

" Stole him ? "

" Not much."

" Picked him up astray ? "

The young surveyor, laughing, shook his head.

" Then how in the name o' seven kingdoms did ye come by him, if ye did n't find him, nor steal him, nor raise him from a colt, nor buy him, nor have him gi'n tew ye ? "

" I borrowed him of a neighbor, and drove him to a show, where the old elephant broke loose and had the handling of him for about a second and a half. The owners of the elephant paid the damages ; and I kept the horse. Nobody thought he would get well; but he is now scarcely lame at all. I can show you the scars where he was hurt."

The two had approached the wagon during this

talk; and now the old man examined the horse with a good deal of curiosity.

"That your dog tew?"

"Yes, sir. Here, Lion!"

"Cost ye suth'n, did n't it, to bring yer animals West with ye?"

"Not a great deal. When my friends wrote for me to come, they said good horses were scarce and high-priced out here, and advised me to bring mine. I could n't leave my dog behind, — could I, old Lion?"

"Who mout your friends be?"

"Mr. and Mrs. Lanman, at North Mills; and Mrs. Lanman's brother, — my boss, as you call him, — Mr. Felton, the surveyor. They came out last year; and last winter they wrote to me, offering me a good chance if I should come. It was in winter; I drove Snowfoot in a cutter, and crossed the Detroit River on the ice just before it broke up. There the sleighing left me; so I sold my cutter, bought a saddle, and made the rest of the journey on horseback. That was rather hard on the dog, but I got the stage-drivers to give him a lift once in a while."

"What did you say your name was?" the old man inquired.

"I don't think I said. But I will say now. My name is Ragdon, — Henry Ragdon. My friends call me Jack."

"And it ain't yer name?"

"O, yes, it is, and yet it is n't! I was brought up to it. My friends like it, and so I keep it." *

"Wal, Jack, — if you 'll rank me with your friends, and le' me call ye so," said the old man, with a cordial grip of his great, flat hand, — " I s'pose we part yer, and say good by. I 'll shoulder my tools, and take a cow-path through the woods ; you 'll find a better road than the one we come by, furder north. Jest keep along the edge of the perairie. I sha' n't forgit this job."

"Nor I," said the young surveyor, with a curious smile.

It was the first work of the kind he had undertaken on his own account, and without assistance ; for which reason he felt not a little proud of it. But he did not tell the old man so.

After parting company with him, he drove in the shade of the woods, along a track so little travelled that the marks of wheels looked like dark ruled lines in the half-trodden grass.

The pleasant summer afternoon was drawing to a close. The peculiar wild scent of the prairie, which seems to increase as the cool evening comes on, filled all the air. The shadows of the forest were stretching in a vast, uneven belt over summit and hollow ; while far away beyond, in seemingly limitless expanse, swept the golden-green undulations of the sunlit hills.

* See "FAST FRIENDS"; also the previous volumes of this series, — "JACK HAZARD AND HIS FORTUNES," "A CHANCE FOR HIMSELF," and "DOING HIS BEST," in which is given a full account of the young surveyor's early life and adventures.

Jack — for I trust we shall also be entitled to call him so — kept his eye out for game, as he drove leisurely along ; stopped once or twice for a rabbit on the edge of the woods ; and, finally, pulled up sharply, as a prairie-hen shot whirring out, almost from under his wheels.

He sprang to his feet and faced about, raising his gun ; but before he could take aim, the bird, at the end of a short, straight flight, dropped into the prairie-grass a few rods away.

Jack followed on foot, holding his piece ready to fire. Knowing the shy habits of the bird, he trampled the grass about the spot where she had alighted, hoping to scare her up. He also sent his dog coursing about ; but Lion, though an intelligent animal, had no scent for birds.

Suddenly, from the very ground between the hunter's feet, with a startling rush and thunder of wings, the hen rose. Up went gun to shoulder. But instantly the dog gave chase, and kept so exactly in the line of flight, that Jack durst not fire.

"You silly boy's dog !" he said ; "don't you know better than that ? You 'll get a stray shot some day, if you run before my gun-barrels in that fashion. Now go to the horse, and stay."

The dog, who had fancied that he was doing good service, dropped ears and tail at this rebuke, and re-tired from the field.

Jack was continuing the hunt, when all at once a strange spell seemed to come over him. It found

him on one foot, and he remained on one foot, poising the other behind him, for several seconds. Then,
softly putting down the lifted leg, and lowering his
gun, he stole swiftly back, in a crouching attitude,
to his wagon by the woodside.

Taking his horse by the bridle, he led him down
into a little hollow. Then, piercing the undergrowth,
he hastened to a commanding position, where, himself hidden by the bushes, he could look off on the
prairie.

His heart beat fast, and his hand shook, as he drew
the bird-shot out of the two barrels of his fowling-
piece, reloading one with buck-shot, the other with
an ounce ball.

All the while his eye kept glancing from his gun
to the shadowy slope of a distant hill, where were
two objects which looked like a deer and a fawn
feeding.

CHAPTER IV.

A DEER HUNT, AND HOW IT ENDED.

THEY were a long way off, — more than half a mile, he thought. Evidently they had not seen him. Though marvellously quick to catch scent or sound, deer have not a fine sense of sight for distant objects.

"They have left the covert early, to go out and feed," thought he. "If not frightened, they will browse around in the hollows there until dark."

He was wondering how he should manage to creep near, and get a shot at the shy creatures, when the dog barked.

"That won't do!" he muttered; and, hurrying to silence Lion, he saw a stranger loitering along the prairie road.

Jack stepped out of the bushes into the hollow, and beckoned.

"I've sighted a couple of deer that I'm trying to get a shot at; if you go over the hill, you'll scare 'em."

The stranger — a slender youth in soiled shirt-sleeves, carrying a coat on his arm — looked at him saucily, with his head on one side and a quid turning in the cheek, and said, —

"Well! and why shouldn't I scare 'em?"

"I can't hinder you, of course; but," said Jack,
"if *you* were hunting, and *I* should be passing by, I
should think it a matter of honor — "

"Honor is an egg that don't hatch in this country,"
interrupted the stranger; and the quid went into the
other cheek, while the head went over on the other
side, as if to balance it. "But never mind; 't ain't
my cut to interfere with another feller's luck. Show
me your deer."

Jack took him through the thickets to his ambush.
There were the deer still feeding; the old one lifting
her head occasionally as if on the lookout for danger.
They seemed to be moving slowly along the slope.

The dark eyes of the strange youth kindled; then
he said, with a low laugh, —

"I 'd like a cut-bore rifle for them fellers! You
never can get 'em with that popgun."

"I believe I can if you 'll help me. You notice
there 's a range of hills between us and them; and
they are on the north slope of one. I 've been surveying a little of the country off south, and I think
you can get around the range that way, and come out
beyond the deer, before they see you. There 's everything in our favor. The wind blows to us from them.
At the first alarm they 'll start for the woods; and
they 'll be pretty sure to keep along in the hollow.
I 'll watch here, and take them as they come in."

Quid and head rolled again; and the strange youth
said jeeringly, with one eye half closed, looking at
Jack, —

2 *   c

"So you expect me to travel a mile or two, and drive the deer in for you?" He then pulled down the nether lid of the half-closed eye, and inquired, somewhat irrelevantly, whether Jack saw anything green there. "Not by this light!" he answered his own question, as he let up his eyelid and snapped his thumb and finger. "Ye can't ketch old birds with chaff. I 've been through the lot. Parley-voo frong-say ?"

Jack regarded him with astonishment, declaring that there was no catch about it. "Only help me, and we will share the game together."

Still the fellow demurred. "I 've walked my legs off to-day already ; you 'll find 'em back in the road here ! Had nothing to eat since morning ; wore myself down lean as a rail ; felt for the last two hours as though there was nothing but my backbone between me and eternity ! No, sir-ree ! I would n't walk that fur out of my way for a herd of deer. If I had a horse to ride I would n't mind."

Jack was greatly excited. He had never yet had a good shot at a deer ; and if, at the end of his day's work, he could carry home a good fat doe, and perhaps a fawn, of his own shooting, it would be a triumph. So, without a moment's reflection, he said,—

"You may ride mine. Then, if you don't want a share of the game, I 'll pay you for your trouble."

The strange youth took time to shift his quid and balance it ; then replied in a manner which appeared provokingly cool to the fiery Jack,—

" I 'll look at him.   Does he ride easy ? "

" Yes.   Hurry ! "

Jack ran down to the horse, led him into the
bushes, where the wagon could be left concealed,
and had already taken him out of the shafts, before
the stranger came lounging to the spot.

" Pull off the harness," said the latter, with the
easy air of ordering a nag at a stable.   " And give
me that blanket out of the buggy.   I don't ride bare-
back for nobody."   And he spat reckless tobacco-
juice.

Jack complied, though angry at the fellow for being so dilatory and fastidious at such a time.   The
strange youth then spread his coat over the blanket,
laid his right hand on it, and his left on bridle and
mane, and with a leap from the ground threw himself astride the horse, — a display of agility which
took Jack by surprise.

" I see you have been on horseback before ! "

" Never in my life," said the stranger, with a gleam
in his dark eyes which belied his words.   And now
Jack noticed that he had a little switch in his hand.

" He won't need urging.   Be sure and ride well
beyond that highest hill before you turn ; and then
come quietly around, so as not to frighten the deer
too much."

The fellow laughed.   " I 've seen a deer before to-
day ! "   And, clapping heels to the horse's sides, he
dashed through the bushes.

Jack followed a little way, and from his ambush

JACK AND THE STRANGE YOUTH.

saw him come out of the undergrowth, strike across
the prairie, and disappear around the range of hills.

The deer were still in sight, stopping occasionally
to feed, and then, with heads in air, moving a few
paces along the slope. Jack waited with breathless
anxiety to see his horseman emerge from among the
hills beyond. Several minutes elapsed; then, though
no horseman appeared, the old deer, startled by
sound or scent of the enemy, threw high her head,

and began to leap, with graceful, undulating movements, along the hillside.

The fawn darted after her, and for a minute they
were hidden from view in a hollow. The stratagem
had so far succeeded. They had started toward the
woods.

Jack, in an ague of agitation, waited for the game
to show itself again, and, by its movements, guide his
own. At length the fawn appeared on the summit
of a low hill, and stopped. The doe came up and
stopped too, with elevated nostrils, snuffing. For a
rifle, in approved hands, there would have been a
chance for a shot. But the game was far beyond the
range of Jack's gun.

To try his nerve, however, he took aim, or, rather,
attempted to take aim. His hands — if the truth
must be confessed — shook so that he could not keep
his piece steady for an instant. Cool fellow enough
on ordinary occasions, he now had a violent attack
of what is called the " buck fever."

Fortunately, the deer had not seen the horseman;
and, while they were recovering from their first
alarm, they gave the young hunter time to subdue,
with resolute good sense, his terrible nervous agitation.

They did not stop to feed any more, but moved
on, with occasional pauses, toward the woods; following the line of the hollows, as Jack had fore-
seen.

All this time the dog lay whining at his young

master's heels. He knew instinctively that there was
sport on foot, and could hardly be kept quiet.

The deer took another and final start, and came
bounding along toward the spot where the wagon
had stood. But for the excitement of the moment,
Jack must have felt a touch of pity at sight of
those two slender, beautiful creatures, so full of life,
making for their covert in the cool woods. But
the hunter's spirit was uppermost. He took aim at
the doe, followed her movements a moment with the
moving gun, then fired. She plunged forward, and
dropped dead.

The fawn, confused by the report and by the doe's
sudden fall, stood for an instant quite still, then
made a few bounds up toward the very spot where
the young hunter was concealed. It stopped again,
within twenty paces of the levelled gun. There it
stood, its pretty spotted side turned toward him, so
fair a mark, and so charming a picture, that for a
moment, excited though he was, he could not have
the heart to shoot. Ah! what is this spirit of de-
struction, which has come down to us from our bar-
barous forefathers, and which gives even good-hearted
boys like Jack a wild joy in taking life?

The dog, rendered ungovernable by the firing of
the gun, made a noise in the thicket. The fawn
heard, and started to run away. The provocation
was too great for our young hunter, and he sent
a charge of buck-shot after it. The fawn did not
fall.

"Take 'em, Lion!" shouted Jack; and out rushed the dog.

The poor thing had been wounded, and the dog soon brought it down. Jack ran after, to prevent a tearing of the hide and flesh. Then he set up a wild yell, which might have been heard a mile away on the prairie, — a call for his horseman, who had not yet reappeared.

Jack dragged the fawn and placed it beside its dam. There lay the two pretty creatures, slaughtered by his hand.

"It can't be helped," thought he. "If it is right to hunt game, it is right to kill it. If we eat flesh, we must take life."

So he tried to feel nothing but pure triumph at the sight. Yet I have heard him say, in relating the adventure, that he could never afterwards think of the dead doe and pretty fawn, lying there side by side, without a pang.

He now backed his buggy out of the woods, set the seat forward in order to make room for the deer behind, and waited for his horse.

"Where can that fellow have gone?" he muttered, with growing anxiety.

He went to a hill-top, to get a good view, and strained his vision, gazing over the prairie. The sun was almost set, and all the hills were darkening, save now and then one of the highest summits.

Over one of these Jack suddenly descried a distant object moving. It was no deer this time, but a horse and rider far away, and going at a gallop — in the wrong direction.

He gazed until they disappeared over the crest, and the faint sundown glory faded from it, and he felt the lonesome night shutting down over the limitless expanse. Then he smote his hands together with fury and despair.

He knew that the horse was his own, and the rider the strange youth in whose hands he had so rashly intrusted him. And here he was, five miles from home, with the darkening forest on one side, and the vast prairie on the other; the dead doe and fawn lying down there on the dewy grass, the empty buggy and harness beside them; and only his dog to keep him company.

CHAPTER V.

THE BOY WITH ONE SUSPENDER.

JACK'S first thought, after assuring himself that his horse was irrevocably gone, was to run for help to the line of settlements on the other side of the grove, where some means of pursuit might be obtained.

He knew that the road which Mr. Wiggett had described could not be much beyond the hollow where his wagon was; and, dashing forward, he soon found it. Then, stopping to give a last despairing look at the billowy line of prairie over which his horse had disappeared, he started to run through the woods.

He had not gone far when he heard a cow-bell rattle, and the voice of a boy shouting. He paused to take breath and listen; and presently with a crashing of bushes three or four horned cattle came pushing their way through the undergrowth, into the open road, followed by a lad without a jacket, with one suspender and a long switch.

"Boy," Jack cried, "how far is it to the nearest house?"

"Our house is jest down through the woods here," replied the boy, stopping to stare.

"How far is that?"

"Not quite so far as it is to Peakslow's house."

" Where is Peakslow's house ? "

" Next house to ours, down the river."

Seeing that this line of questions was not likely to
lead to anything very satisfactory, Jack asked, —

" Can I get a horse of anybody in your neighborhood, — a good fast horse to ride ? "

The boy whipped a bush with his switch, and replied, —

" There ain't any good horses around here, 'thout
't is Peakslow's ; but one of his has got the spring
halt, and t' other 's got the blind staggers ; and he 's
too mean to lend his horses ; and, besides, he went to
Chicago with 'em both this morning."

Jack did not stop to question the probability of a
span thus afflicted being driven on so long a journey ;
but asked if Mr. Wiggett had horses.

" No — yes.   I believe his horses are all oxen,"
replied the boy ; "not very fast or good to ride
either."

Thereupon Jack, losing all patience, cried out, —

" Is n't there a decent nag to be had in this region ? "

" Who said there was n't ? " retorted the boy.

" Where is there one ? "

" We 've got one."

" A horse ? "

" No ; a mare."

" Why did n't you tell me before ? "

" 'Cause you asked for horses ; you did n't say anything about mares."

"Is she good to ride?"

"Pretty good, — though if you make her go much faster 'n she takes a notion to, she's got the heaves so folks 'll think there's a small volcano coming!"

"How fast will she go?"

"As fast as a good slow walk; that's her style," said the boy, and whipped the bushes. "But, come to think, father's away from home, and you'll have to wait till to-morrow night before you can see him, and get him to let you take her."

"Boy," said Jack, tired of the lad's tone of levity, and thinking to interest him by a statement of the facts in the case, "I've been hunting, and a rascal I trusted with my horse has run off with him, and I have a harness and a buggy and a couple of dead deer out there on the prairie."

"Deer?" echoed the lad, pricking up his ears at once. "Did you shoot 'em? Where? Can I go and see 'em?"

Jack was beginning to see the hopelessness of pursuing the horse-thief that night, or with any help to to be had in that region; and he now turned his thoughts to getting the buggy home.

"Yes, boy; come with me," he said.

The boy shouted and switched his stick at the cattle browsing by the wayside, and started them on a smart trot down the road, then hastened with Jack to the spot where the wagon and game had been left, guarded by Lion.

But Jack had another object in view than simply to gratify the lad's curiosity.

"If you will hold up the shafts and pull a little, I'll push behind, and we can take the buggy through the woods. After we get it up out of this hollow, and well into the road, it will be down-hill the rest of the way."

"You want to make a horse of me, do ye?" cried the boy. "I was n't born in a stable!"

"Neither was I," said Jack. "But I don't object to doing a horse's work. I'll pull in the shafts."

"O good!" screamed the boy, making his switch whistle about his head. "And I'll get on the seat and drive!" And he made a spring at the wagon.

But Lion had something to say about that. Having been placed on guard, and not yet relieved, he would permit no hand but his master's to touch anything in his charge. A frightful growl made the boy recoil and go backwards over the dead deer.

"Here, Lion! down with you!" cried Jack, as the excited dog was pouncing on the supposed intruder.

The boy scrambled to his feet, and was starting to run away, in great terror, when Jack, fearing to lose him, called out, —

"Don't run! He may chase you if you do. Now he knows you are my friend, you are safe, only stay where you are."

"Blast his pictur'!" exclaimed the boy. "He's a perfect cannibal! What does anybody want to keep such a savage critter as that for?"

"I had told him to watch. Now he is all right. Come !"

"Me ? Travel with that dog ? I would n't go with him," the boy declared, meaning to make the strongest possible statement, "if 't was a million

UP-HILL WORK.

miles, and the road was full of sugar-candy!" And he backed off warily.

Jack got over the difficulty by sending the dog

on before; and finally, by an offer of money which
would purchase a reasonable amount of sugar-candy,
— enough to pave the short road to happiness, for a
boy of thirteen, — induced him to help lift the deer
into the buggy, and then to go behind and push.

They had hard work at first, getting the wagon up
out of the hollow; and the boy, when they reached
at last the top of the hill, and stopped to rest, declared that there was n't half the fun in it there was
in going a fishing; the justice of which remark Jack
did not question. But after that the way was comparatively easy; and with Jack pulling in the shafts,
his new acquaintance pushing in the rear, and Lion
trotting on before, the buggy went rattling down the
woodland road in lively fashion.

CHAPTER VI.

"LORD BETTERSON'S."

On a sort of headland jutting out from the high timber region into the low prairie of the river bottom, stood a house, known far and near as "Lord Betterson's," or, as it was sometimes derisively called, "Lord Betterson's Castle," the house being about as much a castle as the owner was a lord.

The main road of the settlement ran between it and the woods; while on the side of the river the land swept down in a lovely slope to the valley, which flowed away in a wider and more magnificent stream of living green. It was really a fine site, shaded by five or six young oaks left standing in the spacious door-yard.

The trouble was, that the house had been projected on somewhat too grand a scale for the time and country and, what was worse, for the owner's resources. He had never been able to finish it; and now its weather-browned clapboards, unpainted front pillars, and general shabby, ill-kept appearance, set off the style of architecture in a way to make beholders smile.

"Lord Betterson took a bigger mouthful than he could swaller, when he sot out to build his castle here," said his neighbor, Peakslow.

The proprietor's name — it may as well be explained — was Elisha Lord Betterson. It was thus he always wrote it, in a large round hand, with a bold flourish. Now the common people never will submit to call a man *Elisha*. The furthest they can possibly go will be *'Lisha*, or *'Lishy;* and, ten to one, the tendency to monosyllables will result in *'Lishe*. There had been a feeble attempt among the vulgar to familiarize the public mind with *'Lishe Betterson;* but the name would not stick to a person of so much dignity of character. It was useless to argue that his dignity was mere pomposity; or that a man who, in building a fine house, broke down before he got the priming on, was unworthy of respect; still no one could look at him, or call up his image, and say, conscientiously, "'Lishe Betterson." He who, in this unsettled state of things, taking a hint from the middle name, pronounced boldly aloud, "LORD BETTERSON," was a public benefactor. "Lord Betterson" and "Lord Betterson's Castle" had been popular ever since.

The house, with its door-posts of unpainted pine darkly soiled by the contact of unwashed childish hands, and its unfinished rooms, some of them lathed, but unplastered (showing just the point at which the owner's resources failed), looked even more shabby within than without.

This may have been partly because the house-keeper was sick. She must have been sick, if that was she, the pale, drooping figure, sitting wrapped in

"LORD BETTERSON."

an old red shawl, that summer afternoon. She looked not only sick, but exceedingly discouraged. And no wonder.

At her right hand was an empty cradle; and she held a puny infant in her arms, trying to still its cries. At her left was a lounge, on which lay the helpless form of an invalid child, a girl about eleven years old. The room was comfortless. An old, high-colored piece of carpeting half covered the rough floor; its originally gaudy pattern, out of which all

3   D

but the red had faded, bearing witness to some past stage of family gentility, and serving to set off the surrounding wretchedness.

Tipped back in a chair against the rough and broken laths, his knees as high as his chin, was a big slovenly boy of about seventeen, looking lazily out from under an old ragged hat-rim, pushed over his eyes. Another big, slovenly boy, a year or two younger, sat on the doorstep, whittling quite as much for his own amusement as for that of a little five-year-old ragamuffin outside.

Not much comfort for the poor woman and the sick girl shone from these two indifferent faces. Indeed, the only ray of good cheer visible in that disorderly room gleamed from the bright eyes of a little girl not more than nine or ten years old, — so small, in truth, that she had to stand on a stool by the table, where she was washing a pan of dishes.

"O boys!" said the woman in a feeble, complaining tone, "do, one of you, go to the spring and bring some fresh water for your poor, sick sister."

"It 's Rufe's turn to go for water," said the boy on the doorstep.

"'T ain't my turn, either," muttered the boy tipped back against the laths. "Besides, I 've got to milk the cow soon as Link brings the cattle home. Hear the bell yet, Wad?"

"Never mind, Cecie!" cried the little dish-washer, cheerily. "I 'll bring you some water as soon as I have done these dishes." And, holding her wet hands behind her, she ran to give the young invalid a kiss in the mean while.

Cecie returned a warm smile of love and thanks, and said she was in no hurry. Then the child, stopping only to give a bright look and a pleasant word to the baby, ran back to her dishes.

"I should think you would be ashamed, you two great boys!" said the woman, "to sit round the house and let that child Lilian wait upon you, get your suppers, wash your dishes, and then go to the spring for water for your poor suffering sister!"

"I'm going to petition the Legislature," said Wad, "to have that spring moved up into our back yard; it's too far to go for water. There come the cattle, Rufe."

"Tell Chokie to go and head 'em into the barnyard," yawned Rufe, from his chair. "I wonder nobody ever invented a milking-machine. Wish I had one. Just turn a crank, you know."

"You'll be wanting a machine to breathe with, next," said the little dish-washer.

"Y-a-as," drawled Rufe. "I think a breathing machine would be popular in this family. Children cry for it. Get me the milk-pail, Lill; that's a nice girl!"

"Do get it yourself, Rufus," said the mother. "You'll want your little sister to milk for you, soon."

"I think it belongs to girls to milk," said Rufe. "There's Sal Wiggett, — ain't she smart at it, though ? She can milk your head off! Is that a wagon coming, Wad?"

"Yes!" cried Wad, jumping to his feet with un-usual alacrity. "A wagon without a horse, a fellow pulling in the shafts, and Link pushing behind; coming right into the front yard!"

Rufe also started up at this announcement, and went to the door.

"Hallo!" he said, "had a break-down? What's that in the hind part of your wagon? Deer! a deer and a fawn! Where did you shoot 'em? Where's your horse?"

"Look out, Rufe!" screamed the small boy from behind, rushing forward. "Touch one of these deer, and the dog'll have ye! We've got two deer, but we've lost our horse, — scamp rode him away, — and we want —"

"We do, do we?" interrupted Wad, mockingly. "How many deer did *you* shoot, Link?"

"Well, I helped get the buggy over, anyway! And that's the savagest dog ever was! And — say! will mother let us take the old mare to drive over to North Mills this evening?"

CHAPTER VII.

JACK AT THE "CASTLE."

FOR an answer to this question, the person most interested in it, who had as yet said least, was shown into the house. Rufe and Wad and Link and little Chokie came crowding in after him, all eager to hear him talk of the adventure.

"And, O ma!" cried Link, after Jack had briefly told his story, "he says he will give us the fawn, and pay me besides, if I will go with him to-night, and bring back the old mare in the morning."

"I don't know," said the woman, wrapping her red shawl more closely about her, to conceal from the stranger her untidy attire. "I suppose, if Mr. Betterson was at home, he would let you take the mare. But you know, Lincoln," — turning with a reproachful look to the small boy, — " you have never been brought up to take money for little services. Such things are not becoming in a family like ours."

And in the midst of her distress she put on a complacent smirk, straightened her emaciated form, and sat there, looking like the very ghost of pride, wrapped in an old red shawl.

"Did you speak of Mr. Betterson?" Jack inquired, interested.

"That is my husband's name."

"Elisha L. Betterson?"

"Certainly. You know my husband? He belongs to the Philadelphia Bettersons, — a very wealthy and influential family," said the woman with a simper. "Very wealthy and influential."

"I have heard of your husband," said Jack. "If I am not mistaken, you are Mrs. Caroline Betterson, — a sister of Vinnie Dalton, sometimes called Vinnie Presbit."

"You know my sister Lavinia!" exclaimed Mrs. Betterson, surprised, but not overjoyed. "And you know Mr. Presbit's people?"

"I have never seen them," replied Jack, "but I almost feel as if I had, I have heard so much about them. I was with Vinnie's foster-brother, George Greenwood, in New York, last summer, when he was sick, and she went down to take care of him."

"And I presume," returned Mrs. Betterson, taking another reef in her shawl, "that you heard her tell a good deal about us; things that would no doubt tend to prejudice a stranger; though if all the truth was known she would n't feel so hard towards us as I have reason to think she does."

Jack hastened to say that he had never heard Vinnie speak unkindly of her sister.

"You are very polite to say so," said Mrs. Betterson, rocking the cradle, in which the baby had been

placed. "But I know just what she has said. She
has told you that after I married Mr. Betterson I
felt above my family ; and that when her mother
died (she was not *my* mother, you know, — we are
only half-sisters), I ˙suffered her to be taken and
brought up by the Presbits, when I ought to have
taken her and been as a mother to her, — she was
so much younger than I. She is even younger by
a month or two than my oldest son ; and we have
joked a good deal about his having an aunt younger
than he is."

"Yes," spoke up Rufe, standing in the door; "and
I 've asked a hundred times why we don't ever hear
from her, or write to her, or have her visit us. Other
folks have their aunts come and see 'em. But all
the answer I could ever get was, 'family reasons,
Rufus !' "

"That is it, in a word," said Mrs. Betterson;
"family reasons. I never could explain them ; so I
have never written to poor, dear Lavinia — though,
Heaven knows, I should be glad enough to see her;
and I hope she has forgiven what seemed my hard-
ness ; and — do tell me" (Mrs. Betterson wiped her
eyes) "what sort of a girl is she? how has she
come up ?"

"She is one of the kindest-hearted, most unself-
ish, beautiful girls in the world !" Jack exclaimed.
"I mean, beautiful in her spirit," he added, blush-
ing at his own enthusiasm.

"The Presbits are rather coarse people to bring

up such a girl," said Mrs. Betterson, with a sigh —
of self-reproach, Jack thought.

"But she has a natural refinement which nothing could make her lose," he replied. "Then, it
was a good thing for her to be brought up with
George Greenwood. She owes a great deal to the
love of books he inspired in her. You ought to
know your sister, Mrs. Betterson."

The lady gave way to a flood of tears.

"It is too bad! such separations are unnatural.
Certainly," she went on, "I can't be accused of
feeling above my family now. Mr. Betterson has
had three legacies left him, two since our marriage ;
but he has been exceedingly unfortunate."

"Two such able-bodied boys must be a help and
comfort to you," said Jack.

"Rufus and Wadleigh," said Mrs. Betterson, "are
good boys, but they have been brought up to dreams
of wealth, and they have not learned to take hold
of life with rough hands."

Jack suggested that it might have been better
for them not to have such dreams.

"Yes — if our family is to be brought down to
the common level. But I can't forget, I can't wish
them ever to forget, that they have Betterson blood
in their veins."

Jack could hardly repress a smile as he glanced
from those stout heirs of the Betterson blood to the
evidences of shiftlessness and wretchedness around
them, which two such sturdy lads, with a little less

of the precious article in their veins, might have
done something to remedy.

But his own unlucky adventure absorbed his
thoughts, and he was glad when Link vociferously
demanded if he was to go and catch the mare.

"Yes! yes! do anything but kill me with that
dreadful voice!" replied the mother, waving him
off with her trembling hand. "Don't infer from
what I have said," she resumed, gathering herself
up again with feeble pride, "that we are poor. Mr.
Betterson will come into a large fortune when an
uncle of his dies; and he gets help from him occasionally now. Not enough, however, to enable
him to carry on a farm; and it requires capital,
you are aware, to make agriculture a respectable
profession."

Jack could not forbear another hit at the big boys.

"It requires land," he said; "and that you have.
It also requires bone and muscle; and I see some
here."

"True," simpered Mrs. Betterson. "But their
father has n't encouraged them very much in doing
the needful labors of the farm."

"He has n't set us the example," broke in Rufe,
piqued by Jack's remark. "If he had taken hold
of work, I suppose we should. But while he sits
down and waits for something or somebody to
come along and help him, what can you expect of
us?"

"Our Betterson blood shows itself in more ways
3 *

than one!" said Wad with a grin, illustrating his remark by lazily seating himself once more on the doorstep.

Evidently the boys were sick of hearing their mother boast of the aristocratic family connection. She made haste to change the subject.

"Sickness has been our great scourge. The climate has never agreed with either me or my husband. Then our poor Cecilia met with an accident a year ago, which injured her so that she has scarcely taken a step since."

"An accident done a-purpose!" spoke up Rufe, angrily. "Zeph Peakslow threw her out of a swing, — the meanest trick! They 're the meanest family in the world, and there 's a war between us. I 'm only waiting my chance to pay off that Zeph."

"Rufus!" pleaded the little invalid from the lounge, "you know he could never have meant to hurt me so much. Don't talk of paying him off, Rufus!"

"Cecie is so patient under it all!" said Mrs. Betterson. "She never utters a word of complaint. Yet she does n't have the care she ought to have. With my sick baby, and my own aches and pains, what can I do? There are no decent house-servants to be had, for love or money. O, what would n't I give for a good, neat, intelligent, sympathizing girl! Our little Lilian, here, — poor child! — is all the help I have."

At that moment the bright little dish-washer,

having put away the supper things, and gone to the spring for water, came lugging in a small but brimming pail.

"It is too bad!" replied Jack. "You should have help about the hard work," with another meaning glance at the boys.

"Yes," said Rufe, "we ought to; and we did have Sal Wiggett a little while this summer. But she had never seen the inside of a decent house before. About all she was good for was to split wood and milk the cow."

"O, how good this is!" said the invalid, drinking. "I was so thirsty! Bless you, dear Lill! What should we do without you?"

Jack rose to his feet, hardly repressing his indignation.

"Would you like a drink, sir?" said Lill, taking a fresh cupful from her pail, and looking up at him with a bright smile.

"Thank you, I should very much! But I can't bear the thought of your lugging water from the spring for me."

"Why, Lilie!" said Cecie, softly, "you should have offered it to him first."

"I thought I did right to offer it to my sick sister first," replied Lill, with a tender glance at the lounge.

"You did right, my good little girl!" exclaimed Jack, giving back the cup. He looked from one to the other of the big boys, and wondered how they could witness this scene and not be touched by it. But he only said, "Have these young men too much Betterson blood in them to dress the fawn, if I leave it with you?"

"We'll fall back on our Dalton blood long enough for that," said Wad, taking the sarcasm in good part.

"A little young venison will do Cecie so much good!" said Mrs. Betterson. "You are very kind. But don't infer that we consider the Dalton blood inferior. I was pleased with what you said of Lavinia's native refinement. I feel as if, after all, she was a sister to be proud of."

At this last display of pitiful vanity Jack turned away.

"The idea of such a woman concluding that she may be proud of a sister like Vinnie!" thought he.

But he spoke only to say good by; for just then Link came riding the mare to the door.

She was quickly harnessed to the buggy, while Link, at his mother's entreaty, put on a coat, and made himself look as decent as possible. Then Jack drove away, promising that Link, who accompanied him, should bring the mare back in the morning.

"Mother," said the thoughtful Lill, "we ought to have got him some supper."

"I thought of it," said the sick woman, "but you know we have nothing fit to set before him."

"He won't famish," said Rufe, "with the large supply of sauce which he keeps on hand! Mother,

I wish you would n't ever speak of our Betterson blood again ; it only makes us ridiculous."

Thereupon Mrs. Betterson burst into tears, complaining that her own children turned against her.

" O, bah !" exclaimed Rufe, with disgust, stalking out of the room, banging a milk-pail, and waking the baby. " Be sharpening the knives, Wad, while I milk ; then we 'll dress that fawn in a hurry. Wish the fellow had left us the doe instead."

CHAPTER VIII.

HOW VINNIE MADE A JOURNEY.

LEAVING Jack to drive home the borrowed mare in the harness of the stolen horse, and to take such measures as he can for the pursuit of the thief and the recovery of his property, we have now to say a few words of Mrs. Betterson's younger sister.

Vinnie had perhaps thriven quite as well in the plain Presbit household as she would have done in the home of the ambitious Caroline. The tasks early put upon her, instead of hardening and imbittering her, had made her self-reliant, helpful, and strong, with a grace like that acquired by girls who carry burdens on their heads. For it is thus that labors cheerfully performed, and trials borne with good-will and lightness of heart, give a power and a charm to body and mind.

It was now more than a year since George Greenwood, who had been brought up with her in his uncle's family, had left the farm, and gone to seek his fortune in the city. A great change in the house, and a very unhappy change for Vinnie, had been the result. It was not that she missed her foster-brother so much; but his going out had occasioned the coming in of another nephew, who

brought a young wife with him. The nephew filled
George's place on the farm, and the young wife
showed a strong determination to take Vinnie's
place in the household.

As long as she was conscious of being useful, in
however humble a sphere, Vinnie was contented.
She did her daily outward duty, and fed her heart
with secret aspirations, and kept a brave, bright
spirit through all. But now nothing was left to her
but to contend for her rights with the new-comer, or
to act the submissive part of drudge where she had
almost ruled before. Strife was hateful to her; and
why should she remain where her services were now
scarcely needed ?

So Vinnie lapsed into an unsettled state of mind,
common enough to a certain class of girls of her age,
as well as to a larger class of boys, when the great
questions of practical life confront them: "What am
I to be ? What shall I do for a living ?"

How ardently she wished she had money, so that
she could spend two or three entire years at school !
How eagerly she would have used those advantages
for obtaining an education which so many, who have
them, carelessly throw away ! But Vinnie had nothing — could expect nothing — which she did not
earn.

At one time she resolved to go to work in a fac-
tory ; at another, to try teaching a district school ;
and again, to learn some trade, like that of dress-
maker or milliner. Often she wished for the free-

dom to go out into the world and gain her livelihood like a boy.

In this mood of mind she received two letters. One was from Jack, describing his accidental visit to her sister's family. The other was from Caroline herself, who made that visit the occasion of writing a plaintive letter to her " dear, neglected Lavinia."

Many tears she shed over these letters. The touching picture Jack drew of the invalid Cecie, and the brave little Lilian, and of the sick mother and baby, with Caroline's sad confession of distress, and of her need of sympathy and help, wakened springs of love and pity in the young girl's heart. She forgot that she had anything to forgive. All her half-formed schemes for self-help and self-culture were at once discarded, and she formed a courageous resolution.

"I will go to Illinois," she said, "and take care of my poor sister and her sick children."

Such a journey, from Western New York, was no small undertaking in those days. But she did not shrink from it.

" What !" said Mrs. Presbit, when Vinnie's determination was announced to her, " you will go and work for a sister who has treated you so shamefully all these years ? Only a half-sister, at that ! I 'm astonished at you! I thought you had more sperit."

" For anything she may have done wrong, I am sure she is sorry enough now," Vinnie replied.

"Yes, now she has need of you!" sneered Mrs. Presbit.

"Besides," Vinnie continued, "I ought to go, for. the children's sake, if not for hers. Think of Cecie and the poor baby; and Lilian not ten years old, trying to do the housework! I can do so much for them!"

"No doubt of that; for I must say you are as handy and willing a girl as ever I see. But there's the Betterson side to the family, — two great, lubberly boys, according to your friend's account; a proud, domineering set, I warrant ye! The idee of making a slave of yourself for them! You'll find it a mighty uncomf'table place, mark my word!"

"I hope no more so than the place I am in now, — excuse me for saying it, Aunt Presbit," added Vinnie, in a trembling voice. "It is n't your fault. But you know how things are."

"O, la, yes! *she* wants to go ahead, and order everything; and I think it 's as well to let her, — though she 'll find she can't run over *me*! But I don't blame you the least mite, Vinnie, for feeling sensitive; and if you 've made up your mind to go, I sha' n't hender ye, — I 'll help ye all I can."

So it happened that, only four days after the receipt of her sister's letter, Vinnie, with all her worldly possessions contained in one not very large trunk, bid her friends good by, and, not without misgivings, set out alone on her long journey.

E

She took a packet-boat on the canal for Buffalo. At Buffalo, with the assistance of friends she had made on board the boat, she found the captain of a schooner, who agreed to give her a passage around the lakes to Chicago, for four dollars. There were no railroads through Northern Ohio and across Michigan and Indiana in those days; and although there were steamboats on the lakes, Vinnie found that a passage on one of them would cost more money than she could afford. So she was glad to go in the schooner.

The weather was fine, the winds favored, and the Heron made a quick trip. Vinnie, after two or three days of sea-sickness, enjoyed the voyage, which was made all the more pleasant to her by the friendship of the captain and his wife.

She was interested in all she saw, — in watching the waves, the sailors hauling the ropes, the swelling of the great sails, — in the vessels they met or passed, the ports at which they touched, — the fort, the Indians, and the wonderfully clear depth of the water at Mackinaw. But the voyage grew tiresome toward the close, and her heart bounded with joy when the captain came into the cabin early one morning and announced that they had reached Chicago.

The great Western metropolis was then a town of no more than eight or ten thousand inhabitants, hastily and shabbily built on the low level of the plain stretching for miles back from the lake shore. In a short walk with the captain's wife, Vinnie saw about all of the place she cared to ; noting particularly a load of hay " slewed," or mired, in the mudholes of one of the principal streets; the sight of which made her wonder if a great and flourishing city could ever be built there !

Meanwhile the captain, by inquiry in the resorts of market-men, found a farmer who was going to drive out to the Long Woods settlement that afternoon, and who engaged to come with his wagon to the wharf where the Heron lay, and take off Vinnie and her trunk.

" O, how fortunate ! " she exclaimed. " How good everybody is to me ! Only think, I shall reach my sister's house to-night ! "

CHAPTER IX.

VINNIE'S ADVENTURE.

In due time a rough farm-wagon was backed down upon the wharf, and a swarthy man, with a high, hooked nose, like the inverted prow of a ship, boarded the schooner, and scratched his head, through its shock of stiff, coarse hair, by way of salutation to Vinnie, who came on deck to meet him.

"Do' no 's you 'll like ridin' with me, in a lumber-wagon, on a stiff board seat."

"O, I sha' n't mind!" said Vinnie, who was only too glad to go.

"What part of the settlement ye goin' to?" he asked, as he lifted one end of the trunk, while the captain took up the other.

"To Mr. Betterson's house; Mrs. Betterson is my sister," said Vinnie.

The man dropped his end of the trunk, and turned and glared at her.

"You 've got holt o' the wrong man this time!" he said. "I don't take nobody in my wagon to the house of no sich a man as Lord Betterson. Ye may tell him as much."

"Will you take me to any house near by?" said the astonished Vinnie.

"Not if you 're a connection of the Bettersons, I won't for no money! I 've nothin' to do with that family, but to hate and despise 'em. Tell 'em that too. But they know it a'ready. My name 's Dudley Peakslow."

And, in spite of the captain's remonstrance, the angry man turned his back upon the schooner, and drove off in his wagon.

It took Vinnie a minute to recover from the shock his rude conduct gave her. Then she smiled faintly, and said, —

"It 's too bad I could n't have a ride in his old wagon! But he would n't be very agreeable company, would he?" So she tried to console herself for the disappointment. She had thought all along : "If I can do no better, I will take the stage to North Mills; Jack will help me get over to my sister's from there." And it now seemed as if she might have to take that route.

The schooner was discharging her miscellaneous freight of Eastern merchandise, — dry goods, groceries, hardware, boots and shoes, — and the captain was too much occupied to do anything more for her that afternoon.

She grew restless under the delay; and feeling that she ought to make one more effort to find a conveyance direct to Long Woods, she set off alone to make inquiries for herself.

The first place she visited was a hotel she had noticed in her morning's walk, — the Farmers' Home;

and she was just going away from the door, having met with no success, when a slim youth, carrying his head jauntily on one side, came tripping after her, and accosted her with an apologetic smile and lifted hat.

"Excuse me, — I was told you wanted to find somebody going out to Mr. Betterson's at Long Woods."

"O yes! do you know of anybody I can ride with ?"

"I am in a way of knowing, — why, yes, — I think there is a gentleman going out early to-morrow morning. A gentleman and his daughter. Wife and daughter, in fact. A two-seated wagon ; you might ride on the hind-seat with the daughter. Stopping at the Prairie Flower."

"O, thank you! And can I go there and find them ?"

"I am going that way, and, if you please, I will introduce you," said the youth.

Vinnie replied that, if he would give her their names, she would save him the trouble. For, despite his affability, there was something about him she distrusted and disliked, — an indefinable air of insincerity, and a look out of his eyes of gay vagabondism and dissipation.

He declared that it would be no trouble ; moreover, he could not at that moment recall the names ; so, as there was no help for it, she let him walk by her side.

At the Prairie Flower, — which was not quite so

lovely or fragrant a public-house as the name had led her to expect, — he showed her into a small, dingy sitting-room, up one flight of stairs, and went to speak with the clerk.

"The ladies will be here presently," he said, returning to her in a few minutes. "Meanwhile I thought I would order some refreshments." And he was followed into the room by a waiter bringing a basket of cake and two glasses of wine.

TOO OBLIGING BY HALF.

" No refreshments for me !" cried Vinnie, quickly.

" The other ladies will like some," said the youth, carelessly. " Intimate friends of mine. Just a little cake and sweet wine."

" But you have ordered only two glasses ! And a few minutes ago you could n't think of their names, — those intimate friends of yours !" returned Vinnie, with sparkling eyes.

The youth took up a glass, threw himself back in a chair, and laughed.

" It 's a very uncommon name, — Jenkins ; no, Judkins ; something like that. Neighbors of the Bettersons ; intimate friends of *theirs*, I mean. You think I 'm not acquainted out there ? Ask Carrie ! ask the boys, hi, hi !" — with a giggle and a grimace, as he sipped the wine.

" You do really know my sister Caroline ? " said Vinnie.

The youth set down his glass and stared.

" Your sister! I wondered who in thunder you could be, inquiring your way to Betterson's ; but I never dreamed — Excuse me, I would n't have played such a joke, if I had known !"

" What joke ? " Vinnie demanded.

" Why, there 's no Jenkins, — Judkins, — what did I call their names ? I just wanted to have a little fun, and find you out."

Vinnie trembled with indignation. She started to go.

" But you have n't found *me* out," he said, with an impudent chuckle.

"I've found out all I wish to know of you," said Vinnie, ready to cry with vexation. "I've come alone all the way from my home in Western New York, and met nobody who was n't kind and respectful to me, till I reached Chicago to-day."

The wretch seemed slightly touched by this rebuke; but he laughed again as he finished his glass.

"Well, it was a low trick. But 't was all in fun, I tell ye. Come, drink your wine, and make up; we'll be friends yet. Won't drink? Here goes, then!" And he tossed off the contents of the second glass. "Now we'll take a little walk, and talk over our Betterson friends by the way."

She was already out of the room. He hastened to her side; she walked faster still, and he came tripping lightly after her down the stairs.

Betwixt anger and alarm, she was wondering whether she should try to run away from him, or ask the protection of the first person she met, when, looking eagerly from the doorway as she hurried out, she saw, across the street, a face she knew, and uttered a cry of joy.

"Jack! O Jack!"

It seemed almost like a dream, that it should indeed be Jack, then and there. He paused, glanced up and down, then across at the girlish figure starting toward him, and rushed over to her, reaching out both hands, and exclaiming, —

"Vinnie Dalton! is it you?"

4

In the surprise and pleasure of this unexpected meeting, she forgot all about the slim youth she was so eager to avoid a moment before. When she thought of him again, and looked about her, he had disappeared, having slipped behind her, and skipped back up the stairs with amazing agility at sight of Jack.

CHAPTER X.

JACK AND VINNIE IN CHICAGO.

VINNIE poured out her story to her friend as they walked along the street.

Jack was so incensed, when she came to the upshot of the adventure, that he wished to go back at once and make the slim youth's acquaintance. But she would not permit so foolish a thing.

"It is all over now. What good would it do for you to see him?"

"I don't know; I'd like to tell the scamp what I think of him, if nothing more. He wanted a little fun, did he?" And Jack stood, pale with wrath, looking back at the hotel.

"If it had n't been for him, I might not have seen you," said Vinnie. "Maybe you can't forgive him that!"

Jack looked into her eyes, full of a sweet, mirthful light, and forgot his anger.

"I 'll forgive him the rest, *because* of that. Besides, I 've no time to waste on him. I 'm hunting for my horse."

He had written to Vinnie of his loss; and she was now eager to know if Snowfoot had been heard from.

"Not a hair of him!" said Jack. "I got an old

hunter and trapper to go with me the next day; we struck his trail on the prairie, and after a deal of trouble tracked him to a settler's cabin. There the rogue had stopped, and asked for supper and lodgings, which he promised to pay for in the morning. The man and his wife had gone to bed, but they got up, fed him and the horse, and then made him up a bed on the cabin floor. He pretended to be very careful of his horse, and he had to go out and make sure that he was all right before he went to bed; and that was the last they saw of him. He bridled Snowfoot, and rode off so slyly that they never knew which way he went. He had struck the travelled road, and there we lost all trace of him. I went on to Joliet, and looked along the canal, and set stablemen to watch for him, while my friend took the road to Chicago; but neither of us had any luck. I've hunted all about the country for him; and now, for a last chance, I've come to Chicago myself."

"How long have you been here?" Vinnie asked.

"Only about two hours; and I must go back to-morrow. I've not much hope of finding Snowfoot here; but as I had a chance to ride in with a neighbor, I thought best to take advantage of it. Lucky I did! Why didn't you write and let somebody know you were coming?"

"I did write to my sister; but I didn't expect anybody to meet me here in Chicago, since I couldn't tell just when I should arrive."

"Where are you stopping?"

"On board the schooner that brought me. She is lying quite near here, at a wharf in the river."

"Can you stay on board till to-morrow?"

Vinnie thought the captain and his wife would be glad to keep her.

"Though it is n't very nice," she added, "now that · they are discharging the cargo."

"Perhaps you had better go to the Farmers' Home, where my friend and I have put up," said Jack.   ·

"You at the Farmers' Home! Why could n't I have known it?" said Vinnie. "It was there I went to inquire for Long Woods people, and met that scapegrace. When do you go home?"

"We start early to-morrow morning. You can go with us as well as not, — a good deal better than not!" said the overjoyed Jack. "Nothing but a little load of groceries. You shall go home with me to North Mills; Mrs. Lanman will be glad to see you. Then I'll drive you over to Long Woods in three or four days."

"Three or four days!" exclaimed Vinnie, not daring to be as happy as these welcome words might have made her. "I should like much to visit your friends; but I must get to my sister's as soon as possible."

Jack's face clouded.

"Vinnie, I'm afraid you don't know what you have undertaken. I can't bear the thought of your going into that family. Why do you? The Lanmans will be delighted to have you stay with them."

"O, but I must go where I am needed," Vinnie answered. "And you must n't say a word against it. You must help me, Jack!"

"They need you enough, Heaven knows, Vinnie!" Jack felt that he ought not to say another word to discourage her, so he changed the subject. "Which way now is your schooner?"

Vinnie said she would show him; but she wished to buy a little present for the captain's wife on the way. As they passed along the street, she made him tell all he knew of her sister's family; and then asked if he had heard from George Greenwood lately.

"Only a few days ago he sent me a magazine with a long story of his in it, founded on our adventure with the pickpockets," replied Jack. "He writes me a letter about once a month. You hear from him, of course?"

"O yes. And he sends me magazines. He has wonderful talent, don't you think so?"

And the two friends fell to praising the absent George.

"I wonder if you have noticed one thing?" said Vinnie.

"What, in particular?"

"That Grace Manton has been the heroine of all his last stories."

"I fancied I could see you in one or two of them," replied Jack.

"Perhaps. But I am not the heroine; I am only the goody-goody girl," laughed Vinnie. "When you see beauty, talent, accomplishments, — that's Grace. I am glad they are getting on so well together."

"So am I!" said Jack, with an indescribable look at the girl beside him.

"Mr. Manton is dead, — I suppose you know it," said Vinnie.

Jack knew it, and was not sorry; though he had much to say in praise of the man's natural talents, which dissipation had ruined.

The purchase made, they visited the schooner, where it was decided that Vinnie should remain on board. Jack then left her, in order to make the most of his time looking about the city for his horse.

He continued his search, visiting every public stable, making inquiries of the hostlers, and nailing up or distributing a small hand-bill he had had printed, offering a reward of twenty dollars for "a light, reddish roan horse, with white forefeet, a conspicuous scar low down on the near side, just behind the shoulder, and a smaller scar on the off hip."

In the mean time he kept a sharp lookout for roan horses in the streets. But all to no purpose. There were roan horses enough, but he could see and hear nothing of the particular roan he wanted.

In the evening he went to see Vinnie on board the schooner, and talked of his ill success.

"A light roan? that's a kind of gray, ain't it?" said the captain of the Heron. "That bearish fellow from Long Woods, who would n't take into his wagon anybody connected with the Bettersons—"

"Dudley Peakslow,—I sha' n't soon forget his name!" said Vinnie.

"He drove such a horse," said the captain; "though I did n't notice the forefeet or any scars."

Jack laughed, and shook his head.

"That's what everybody says. But the scars and forefeet are the main points in my case. I would n't give a cent for a roan horse without 'em!" Then he changed the subject. "It's a beautiful night, Vinnie; let's go for a little stroll on the lake shore, and forget all about roans,—light roans, dark roans, white feet, black, blue, green, yellow feet! Perhaps your friends will go with us."

Jack hoped they would n't, I regret to say. But the night was so pleasant, and the captain's wife had become so attached to Vinnie, that she persuaded her husband to go.

The lake shore was charming; for in those early days it had not been marred by breakwaters and docks. The little party strolled along the beach, with the sparkling waves dashing at their feet, and the lake spread out before them, vast, fluctuating, misty-gray, with here and there a white crest tossing in the moon.

Singing snatches of songs with Vinnie, telling stories with the captain, skipping pebbles on the

lake, — ah, how happy Jack was! He was glad,
after all, that they had all come together, since
there was now no necessity of Vinnie's hastening
back to the schooner, to prevent her friends from
sitting up for her.

"I've been in this port fifty times," said the captain, " but I've never been down here before, neither
has my wife; and I'm much obliged to you for
bringing us."

"I like the lake," said his wife, " but I like it best
from shore."

"O, so do I!" said Vinnie, filled with the peace
and beauty of the night.

It was late when they returned to the schooner.
There Jack took his leave, bidding Vinnie hold herself in readiness to be taken off, with her trunk, in
a grocer's wagon early the next morning.

CHAPTER XI.

JACK'S NEW HOME.

IN due time the wagon was driven to the wharf; and Vinnie, parting from the captain and his wife with affectionate good-byes, rode out in the freshness of the morning across the great plain stretching back from the city.

The plain left behind, groves and streams and high prairies were passed; all wearing a veil of romance to the eye of the young girl, which saw everything by its own light of youth and hope.

But the roads were in places rough and full of ruts; the wagon was pretty well loaded; and Vinnie was weary enough, when, late in the afternoon, they approached the thriving new village of North Mills.

"Here we come to Lanman's nurseries," said Jack, as they passed a field of rich dark soil, ruled with neat rows of very young shrubs and trees. "Felton is interested in the business with him; and I work for them a good deal when we 've no surveying to do. They 're hardly established yet; but they 're sure of a great success within a few years, for all this immense country must have orchards and garden fruits, you know. Ah, there 's Lion!"

The dog came bounding to the front wheels,

whining, barking, leaping up, wagging his tail, and finally rolling over in the dirt, to show his joy at seeing again his young master.

The Lanman cottage was close by; and there in the door was its young mistress, who, warned by the dog of the wagon's approach, had come out to see if Jack's horse was with him.

"No news of Snowfoot?" she said, walking to the gate as the wagon stopped.

"Not a bit. But I've had good luck, after all. For here is — who do you suppose? Vinnie Dalton! Vinnie, this is the friend you have heard me speak of, Mrs. Annie Felton Lanman."

Vinnie went out of the wagon almost into the arms of Annie; so well had both been prepared by Jack to know and to love each other.

Of course the young girl received a cordial welcome; and to her the little cottage seemed the most charming in the world. It contained few luxuries, but everything in it was arranged with neatness and taste, and exhaled an atmosphere of sweetness and comfort which mere luxury can never give.

"Lion has been watching for you with the anxiety of a lover all the afternoon," Mrs. Lanman said to Jack, as, side by side, with Vinnie between them, they walked up the path to the door. "And he is jealous because you don't give him more attention."

"Not jealous; but he wants to be introduced to Vinnie. Here, old fellow!"

Vinnie was delighted to make acquaintance with

the faithful dog, and listened eagerly to Annie's praise of him as they entered the house.

"He is useful in doing our errands," said Mrs. Lanman. "If I wish to send him to the grocery for anything, I write my order on a piece of paper, put it into a basket, and give the basket to him, just lifting my finger, and saying, 'Go to the grocery, go to the grocery,' twice; and he never makes a mistake. To-day, Jack, for the first time, he came home without doing his errand."

"Why, Lion! I'm surprised at you!" said Jack; while Lion lay down on the floor, looking very much abashed.

"I sent him for butter, which we wanted to use at dinner. As I knew, when he came back, that the order, which I placed in a dish in the basket, had not been touched, I sent him again. 'Don't come home,' I said, 'till somebody gives you the butter.' He then went, and didn't return at all. So, as dinner-time came, I sent my brother to look after him. He found the grocery closed, and Lion waiting with his basket on the steps."

"The grocer is sick," Jack explained; "his son had gone to town with me; and so the clerk was obliged to shut up the store when he went to din- ner." And he praised and patted Lion, to let him know that they were not blaming him for his fail- ure to bring the butter.

"One day," said Annie, "he had been sent to the butcher's for a piece of meat. On his way home he saw a small dog of his acquaintance engaged in a desperate fight with a big dog, — as big as Lion himself. At first he ran up to them much excited; then he seemed to remember his basket of meat. He could n't go into the fight with that, and he was too prudent to set it down in the street. For a moment he looked puzzled; then he ran to the grocery, which was close by, — the same place where we send him for things; but instead of holding up his basket before one of the men, as he does when his errand is with them, he went and set it carefully down behind a barrel in a corner. Then he rushed out and gave the big dog a severe punishing. The men in the grocery watched him; and, knowing that he would return for the basket, they hid it in another place, to see what he would do. He went back into the store, to the corner behind the barrel, and appeared to be in great distress. He snuffed and whimpered about the store for a while, then ran up to the youngest of the men — "

" Horace, — the young fellow who came out with us to-day," commented Jack. "He is full of his fun; and Lion knew that it would be just like him to play such a trick."

— " He ran up to Horace," Annie continued, " and barked furiously ; and became at last so fiercely threatening, that it was thought high time to give him the basket. Lion took it and ran home in extraordinary haste ; but it was several days before he would have anything more to do with Horace."

"Who can say, after this, that dogs do not think?"
said the admiring Vinnie.

"Mr. Lanman thinks he has some St. Bernard
blood," said Jack, "and that is what gives him his
intelligence. He knows just what we are talking
about now; and see! he hardly knows whether to
be proud or ashamed. I don't approve of his fighting, on ordinary occasions; and I 've had to punish
him for it once or twice. The other evening, as
I was coming home from a hunt after my horse, I
saw two dogs fighting near the saw-mill."

Jack had got so far when Lion, who had seemed
to take pleasure in being in the room till that moment, got up very quietly and went out with drooping ears and tail.

"He knows what is coming, and does n't care to
hear it. There 's a little humbug about Lion, as
there is about the most of us. It was growing dark,
and the dogs were a little way off, and I was n't
quite sure of Lion; but some boys who saw the fight
told me it *was* he, and I called to him. But what do
you think he did? Instead of running to greet me,
as he always does when he sees me return after an
absence, he fought a little longer, then pretended to
be whipped, and ran around the saw-mill, followed by
the other dog. The other dog came back, but Lion
did n't. I was quite surprised, when I got home, to
see him rush out to meet me in an ecstasy of delight, as if he then saw me for the first time. His
whole manner seemed to say, 'I am tickled to see

you, Jack! and if you think you saw me fighting the sawyer's dog just now, you're much mistaken.' I don't know but I might have been deceived, in spite of the boys; but one thing betrayed him, — he was wet. In order to get home before me, without passing me on the road, he had swum the river."

"Now you must tell the story of the chickens," said Annie.

"Another bit of humbug," laughed Jack. "Our neighbors' chickens trouble us by scratching in our yard, and I have told Lion he must keep them out. But I noticed that sometimes, even when he had been on guard, there were signs that the chickens had been there and scratched. So I got Mrs. Lanman to watch him for two or three days, while he watched the chickens. Now Lion is very fond of company; so, as soon as I was out of sight, he would let the chickens come in, and scratch and play all about him, while he would lie with his nose on his paws and blink at them as good-naturedly as possible. But he kept an eye out for me all the while, and the moment I came in sight he would jump up, and go to frightening away the chickens with a great display of vigor and fidelity. So you see, Lion isn't a perfect character, by any means. I could tell you a good deal more about his peculiarities; but I think you are too tired now to listen to any more dog stories."

Jack carried Vinnie's trunk to a cosey little room; and there she had time to rest and make herself presentable, before Mrs. Lanman came to tell her that tea was ready.

"See here, Vinnie, a minute!" said Jack, peeping from a half-opened door. "Don't make a noise!" he whispered, as if there were a great mystery within. "I'll show you something very precious."

Mrs. Lanman followed, smiling, as Jack led Vinnie to a crib, lifted a light veil, and discovered a lovely little cherub of a child, just opening its soft blue eyes, and stretching out its little rosy hands, still dewy with sleep.

"O how sweet!" said Vinnie, thrilled with love and tenderness at the sight.

"She has a smile for you, see!" said the pleased young mother.

Of course Vinnie had never seen so pretty a baby, such heavenly eyes, or such cunning little hands.

"The hands are little," said Jack, in a voice which had an unaccustomed tremor in it; "but they are stronger than a giant's; they have hold of all our heart-strings."

"I never knew a boy so fond of a baby as Jack is," said Annie.

"O, but I should n't be so fond of any other baby!" Jack replied, bending down to give the little thing a fond caress.

As they went out to tea, there was a happy light on all their faces, as if some new, deep note of harmony had just been struck in their hearts.

At tea Vinnie made the acquaintance of Annie's

brother and husband, and Jack's friends, Mr. Forrest Felton and Mr. Percy Lanman, and — so pleasant and genial were their ways — felt at home in their presence at once. This was a great relief to her; for she felt very diffident at meeting men whom she had heard Jack praise so highly.

Any one could see that Vinnie was not accustomed to what is called society; but her native manners were so simple and sincere, and there was such an air of fresh, young, joyous, healthy life about her, that she produced an effect upon beholders which the most artificially refined young lady might have envied.

Jack watched her and Annie a good deal slyly; and there was in his expression a curious mixture of pride and anxiety, as if he were trying to look at each with the other's eyes, and thinking how they must like each other, yet having some fears lest they might not see all he saw to admire.

Vinnie was made to talk a good deal of her journey; and she told the story with so much simplicity, speaking with unfeigned gratitude and affection of the friendships she had made, and touching with quiet mirthfulness upon the droll events, as if she hardly knew herself that they were droll, that all — and especially Jack — were charmed.

But she had not the least idea of "showing off." Indeed, she thought scarcely at all of what others thought of her; but said often to herself, "What a beautiful home Jack has, and what pleasant companions!"

After tea she must see more of the baby; then Jack wanted to show her the greenhouses and the nurseries; and then all settled down to a social evening.

"Vinnie is pretty tired," said Jack, "and I think a little music will please her better than anything else."

And so a little concert was got up for her entertainment.

Forrest Felton was a fine performer on the flute; Mr. Lanman played the violin, and his wife the piano; and they discoursed some excellent music. Then, still better, there was singing. The deep-chested Forrest had a superb bass voice; Lanman a fine tenor; Annie's voice was light, but exceedingly sweet and expressive; and they sang several pieces together, to her own accompaniment on the piano. Then Lanman said, —

"Now it is your turn, Jack."

"But you know," replied Jack, "I never play or sing for anybody, when your wife or Forrest is present."

"True; but you can dance."

"O yes! a dance, Jack!" cried Annie.

Vinnie clapped her hands. "Has Jack told you," she said, "how, on the steamboat going from Albany to New York, after they had had their pockets picked, he and George Greenwood collected a little money, — George playing the flute and Jack dancing, for the amusement of the passengers?"

Jack laughed, and looked at his shoes.

"Well, come to the kitchen, where there's no carpet on the floor, and I'll give you what I call the 'Canal Driver's Hornpipe.' Bring your flute, Forrest."

So they went to the kitchen; and all stood, while Jack, with wild grace of attitude and wonderful ease and precision of movement, performed one of his most difficult and spirited dances.

When it was ended, in the midst of the laughter and applause, he caught up a hat, and gayly passed it around for pennies. But while the men were feeling in their pockets, he appeared suddenly to remember where he was.

"Beg pardon," he cried, sailing his hat into a corner, and whirling on his heel, — "I forgot myself; I thought I was on the deck of the steamboat!"

This closed the evening's entertainment.

When Vinnie, retiring to her room, laid her head on the pillow, she thought of the night before and of this night, and asked her heart if it could ever again know two evenings so purely happy.

Then a great wave of anxiety swept over her mind, as she thought of the other home, to which she must hasten on the morrow.

CHAPTER XII.

VINNIE'S FUTURE HOME.

A LIVELY sensation was produced, the next forenoon, when a youth and a girl, in a one-horse wagon,
with a big dog and a small trunk, arrived at Lord
Betterson's " castle."

Link dashed into the house, screaming, " They 've
come! they 've come!"

" Who has come?" gasped poor Mrs. Betterson,
with a start of alarm, glancing her eye about the
disordered room.

" Jack What's-his-name! the fellow that shot the
deer and lost his horse. It 's Aunt Lavinny with
him, I bet!"

And out the boy rushed again, to greet the new-
comers.

Lill, who was once more washing dishes at the
table, stepped down from her stool, and ran out too,
drying her fingers on her apron by the way. Five-
year-old Chokie got up from his holes in the earth
by the doorstep, and stood with dangling hands and
sprawling fingers, grinning, dirty-faced.

Vinnie, springing to the ground with Jack's help,
at the side door caught Lill in her arms, and gave
her an ardent kiss.

LINK DOES N'T CARE TO BE KISSED. — Page 93.

"I have heard of you!" she said; for she had recognized the bright, wistful face.

"Dear auntie!" said the child, with tears and smiles of joy, "I 'm so glad you 've come!"

"Here is Link — my friend Link," said Jack. "Don't overlook him."

"I 've heard a good deal about you too, Link!" said Vinnie, embracing him also, but not quite so impulsively.

"Ye need n't mind kissing me!" said Link, bashfully turning his face. "And as for him," — as she passed on to the five-year-old, — "that 's Chokie; he 's a reg'lar prairie gopher for digging holes; you won't find a spot on him big as a sixpence clean enough to kiss, I bet ye two million dollars!"

Vinnie did not accept the wager, convinced, probably, that she would lose it if she did. As she bent over the child, however, the report of a kiss was heard, — a sort of shot in the air, not designed to come very near the mark.

"I 'm didding a well," said Chokie, in a solemn voice, "so the boys won't have to do to the spring for water."

Mrs. Betterson tottered to the door, convulsively wrapping her red shawl about her.

"Lavinia! Is it sister Lavinia?"

At sight of her, so pale and feeble, Vinnie was much affected. She could hardly speak; but, supporting the emaciated form in her strong, embracing arms, she led her back into the house.

"You are so good to come!" said Mrs. Betterson, weeping, as she sank in her chair. "I am worse than when I wrote to you; and the baby is no better; and Cecie — poor Cecie! though she can sit up but little, she does more than any of us for the sick little thing."

Vinnie turned to the lounge, where Cecie, with the baby in her arms, lay smiling with bright, moist eyes upon the new-comer. She bent over and kissed them both; and, at sight of the puny infant, — so pitiful a contrast to Mrs. Lanman's fair and healthy child, — she felt her heart contract with grief and her eyes fill.

Then, as she turned away with an effort at self-control, and looked about the room, she must have noticed, too, the painful contrast between Jack's home and this, which was to be hers; and have felt a sinking of the heart, which it required all her strength and courage to overcome.

"We are not looking fit to be seen; I know it, Lavinia!" sighed Mrs. Betterson. "But you'll excuse it — you've already excused so many things in the past! It seems a dreadful, unnatural thing for *our* family to be so — so very — yet don't think we are absolutely reduced, Lavinia. Mr. Betterson's connections, as everybody knows, are very wealthy and aristocratic, and they are sure to do something for him soon. This is my husband, sister Lavinia." And, with a faint simper of satisfaction, she looked up at a person who just then entered from an adjoining room.

He was a tall, well-made man, who looked (Vinnie could not help thinking) quite capable of doing something for himself. He might have been called fine-looking, but that his fine looks, like his gentility, of which he made a faded show in his dress and manners, appeared to have gone somewhat to seed. He greeted Vinnie with polite condescension, said a few commonplace words, settled his dignified chin in his limp dicky, which was supported by a high, tight stock (much frayed about the edges), and went on out of the house.

"Now you have seen him!" whispered Mrs. Betterson, as if it had been a great event in Vinnie's life. "Very handsome, and perfectly well-bred, as you observe. Not at all the kind of man to be neglected by his family, aristocratic as they are; do you think he is? Yes, my dear Lavinia," she added, with a sickly smile, "you have seen a real, live Betterson!"

These evidences of a foolish pride surviving affliction made poor Vinnie more heartsick than anything else; and for a moment the brave girl was almost overcome with discouragement.

In the mean while the real, live Betterson walked out into the yard, where Jack — who had not cared to follow Vinnie into the house — was talking with Link.

"Will you walk in, sir?" And the stately Betterson neck bent slightly in its stiff stock.

"No, I thank you," replied Jack. "But I suppose this trunk goes in."

"Ah! to be sure.   Lincoln," — with a wave of the aristocratic Betterson hand, — "show the young man where to put the trunk.   He can take it to Cecie's room."

"I can, can I?   That's a privilege!" thought Jack.   He was perfectly willing to be a porter, or anything else, in a good cause; and it was a delight for him to do Vinnie a service; but why did the noble Betterson stand there and give directions about the trunk, in that pompous way, instead of taking hold of one end of it?   Jack, who had a lively spirit, and a tongue of his own, was prompted to say something sarcastic, but he wisely forbore.

"I'll place it here for the present," he said, and set the trunk down by the doorstep.   He thought it would be better for him to see Vinnie and bid her good-by a little later, after the meeting between the sisters should be well over; so he turned to Link, and asked where his big brothers were.

"I d'n' know," said Link; "guess they're down in the lot hunting prairie hens."

"Let's go and find 'em," said Jack.

Both Link and Lion were delighted with this proposal, and they set off in high glee, boy and dog capering at each side of the more steady-going Jack.

CHAPTER XIII.

WHY JACK DID NOT FIRE AT THE PRAIRIE CHICKEN.

"A WELL?" said Jack, as they passed a curb behind the house. "I thought you had to go to the spring for water."

"So we do," said Link.

"Why don't you use the well?"

"I d'n' know; 't ain't good for anything. 'T ain't deep enough."

"Why was n't it dug deeper?"

"I d'n' know; father got out of patience, I guess, or out of money. 'T was a wet time, and the water came into it, so they stunned it up; and now it 's dry all summer."

They passed a field on the sunny slope, and Jack said, "What 's here?"

"I d'n' know; 't was potatoes, but it 's run all to weeds."

"Why did n't you hoe them?"

"I d'n' know; folks kind o' neglected 'em, till 't was too late."

Beyond the potatoes was another crop, which the weeds, tall as they were, could not hide.

"Corn?" said Jack.

"Meant for corn," replied Link. "But the cattle

5   G

and hogs have been in it, and trampled down the rows."

"I should think so! They look like the last rows of summer!" Jack said. "Why don't you keep the cattle and hogs out?"

"I d'n' know; 't ain't much of a fence; hogs run under and cattle jump over."

"Plenty of timber close by,—why don't your folks make a better fence?"

"I d'n' know; they don't seem to take a notion."

Jack noticed that the river was quite near, and asked if there was good boating.

"I d'n' know,—pretty good, only when the water's too low."

"Do you keep a boat?"

"Not exactly,—we never had one of our own," said Link. "But one came floating down the river, and the boys nabbed that. A fust-rate boat, only it leaked like a sieve."

"Leaked? Does n't it leak now?"

"No?" said Link, stoutly. "They hauled it up, and last winter they worked on it, odd spells, and now it don't leak a drop."

Jack was surprised to hear of so much enterprise in the Betterson family, and asked,—

"Stopped all the leaks in the old boat! They puttied and painted it, I suppose?"

"No, they did n't."

"Calked and pitched it, then?"

"No, they did n't."

"What did they do to it?"

"Made kindling-wood of it," said Link, laughing, and hitching up his one suspender.

Jack laughed too, and changed the subject.

"Is that one of your brothers with a gun?"

"That's Wad; Rufe is down on the grass."

"What sort of a crop is that,— buckwheat?"

Link grinned. "There's something funny about that! Ye see, a buckwheat-lot is a great place for prairie hens. So one day I took the old gun, and the powder and shot you gave me for carrying you home that night, and went in, and scared up five or six, and fired at 'em, but I did n't hit any. Wad came along and yelled at me. 'Don't you know any better'n to be trampling down the buckwheat?' says he. 'Out of there, quicker!' And he took the gun away from me. But he'd seen one of the hens I started light again on the edge of the buckwheat; so he went in to find her. 'You're trampling the buckwheat yourself!' says I. 'No, I ain't,' says he, —'I step between the spears; and I'm coming out in a minute.' He stayed in, though, about an hour, and went all over the patch, and shot two prairie chickens. Then Rufe came along, and he was mad enough, 'cause Wad was treading down the buckwheat. 'Come out of that!' says he, 'or I'll go in after ye, and put that gun where you won't see it again.' So Wad came out; and the sight of his chickens made Rufe's eyes shine. 'Did ye shoot *them* in the buckwheat?' says he. 'Yes,' says Wad;

'and I could shoot plenty more; the patch is full of
'em.' Rufe said he wanted the gun to go and shoot
ducks with, on the river; but he did n't find any
ducks, and coming along back he thought he would
try *his* luck in the buckwheat, — treading between
the spears! He had shot three prairie chickens,
when father came along, and scolded him, and made
him come out. 'I 've heard you fire twenty times,'
says father; 'you 're wasting powder and ruining the
crop. Let *me* take the gun.' 'But *you* must n't ruin
the crop,' says Rufe. Father 's a splendid shot, —
can drop a bird every time, — only he don't like to
go hunting very often. He thought 't would pay for
him to go through the patch *once;* besides, he said,
if the birds were getting the buckwheat, we might as
well get the birds. He thought *he* could tread between the spears! Well, since then," said Link,
"we 've just made a hunting-ground of that patch,
always treading between the spears till lately; now
it 's got so trampled it never 'll pay to cut it; so we
just put it through. See that hen!"

There was a sound of whirring wings, — a flash, a
loud report, a curl of smoke, — a broken-winged
grouse shooting down aslant into the buckwheat, and
a young hunter running to the spot.

"That 's the way he does it," said Rufe, getting up
from the grass.

He greeted Jack good-naturedly, inquired about
Snowfoot, heard with surprise of Vinnie's arrival,
and finally asked if Jack would like to try his hand
at a shot.

"I should," replied Jack, "if it was n't for treading down your buckwheat."

"That 's past caring for," said Rufe, with a laugh.
"Here, Wad, bring us the gun."

"Is that your land the other side of the fence?"
Jack asked.

"That lot belongs to old 'Peakslow," said Rufe,
speaking the name with great contempt. "And he
pretends to claim a big strip this side too. That 's
what caused the feud between our families."

"He hates you pretty well, I should judge," replied
Jack; and he told the story, as Vinnie had told it to
him, of her encounter with Peakslow on the deck of
the schooner.

"He 's the ugliest man!" Rufe declared, reddening
angrily. "You may thank your stars you 've nothing
to do with him. Now take the gun," — Wad had by
this time brought it, — "go through to the fence and
back, and be ready to fire the moment a bird rises.
Keep your dog back, and look out and not hit one of
Peakslow's horses, the other side of the fence."

"He brought home a new horse from Chicago a
day or two ago," said Wad; "and he 's just been out
there looking at him and feeling for ringbones. If
he 's with him now, and if you *should* happen to
shoot *one* of 'em, I hope it won't be the horse!"

Jack laughed, and started to go through the buckwheat. He had got about half-way, when a hen rose
a few feet from him, at his right. He was not much
accustomed to shooting on the wing; and it is much

harder to hit birds rising suddenly, at random, in that
way, than when they are started by a trained dog.
But good luck made up for what he lacked in skill ;

SHOT ON THE WING.

and at his fire the hen dropped fluttering in the grass
that bordered the buckwheat.

"I 'll pick her up!" cried Link ; and he ran to do

so; while Wad carried Jack the powder and shot for another load.

"But I ought not to use up your ammunition in this way!" Jack protested.

"I guess you can afford to," replied Wad. "It was mostly bought with money we sold that fawn-skin for."

Jack was willing enough to try another shot; and, the piece reloaded, he resumed his tramp.

He had nearly reached the fence, when a bird rose between it and him, and flew over Peakslow's pasture. Jack had brought the gun to his shoulder, and was about to pull the trigger, when he remembered Peak-slow's horses, and stopped to give a hasty glance over the fence.

Down went the gun, and Jack stood astonished, the bird forgotten, and his eyes fixed on an object beyond.

What Wad said of their neighbor having brought out a new horse from Chicago, together with what the captain of the Heron said of one of Peakslow's span being a light roan, rushed through his thoughts. He ran up to the fence, and looked eagerly over; then gave a shout of joy.

After all his futile efforts to find him, — chasing about the country, offering rewards, scattering hand-bills, — there was the lost horse, the veritable Snow-foot, grazing quietly in the amiable Mr. Peakslow's pasture!

CHAPTER XIV.

SNOWFOOT'S NEW OWNER.

JACK left the gun standing by the fence, leaped over, gave a familiar whistle, and called, "Come, Snowfoot! Co' jock! co' jock!"

There were two horses feeding in the pasture, not far apart. But only one heeded the call, lifted head, pricked up ears, and answered with a whinny. It was the lost Snowfoot, giving unmistakable signs of pleasure and recognition, as he advanced to meet his young master.

Jack threw his arms about the neck of his favorite, and hugged and patted and I don't know but kissed him; while the Betterson boys went up to the fence and looked wonderingly over.

In a little while, as they did not venture to go to him, Jack led Snowfoot by the forelock up to the rails, which they had climbed for a better view.

"Is he your horse?" they kept calling to him.

"Don't you see?" replied Jack, when he had come near enough to show the white feet and the scars; and his face gleamed with glad excitement. "Look! he and the dog know each other!"

It was not a Betterson, but a Peakslow style of fence, and Lion could not leap it; but the two animals touched noses, with tokens of friendly recognition, between the rails.

"I never expected such luck!" said Jack. "I 've not only found my horse, but I 've saved the reward offered."

"You have n't got him yet," said Rufe. "I guess Peakslow will have something to say about that."

"What he says won't make much difference. I 've only to prove property, and take possession. A stolen horse is the owner's, wherever he finds him. But of course I 'll act in a fair and open way in the matter; I 'll go and talk with Peakslow, and if he 's a reasonable man —"

"Reasonable!" interrupted Wad. "He holds a sixpence so near to his eye, that it looks bigger to him than all the rest of the world; he can't see reason, nor anything else."

"I 'll make him see it. Will you go and introduce me?"

"You 'd better not have one of our family introduce you, if you want to get anything out of Dud Peakslow!" said Rufe. "We 'll wait here."

Jack got over the fence, and walked quickly along on the Betterson side of it, followed by Lion, until he reached the road. A little farther down was a house; behind the house was a yard; and in the yard was a swarthy man with a high, hooked nose, pulling a wheel off a wagon, the axletree of which, on that side, was supported by a propped rail. Close by was a boy stirring some grease in a pot, with a long stick.

5*

Jack waited until the man had got the wheel off and rested it against the wagon ; then said, —

" Is this Mr. Peakslow ? "

" That happens to be my name," replied the man, scarcely giving his visitor a glance, as he turned to take the stick out of the grease, and to rub it on the axletree.

The boy, on one knee in the dirt, holding the grease-pot to catch the drippings, looked up and grinned at Jack.

" I should like a few minutes' talk with you, Mr. Peakslow, when you are at leisure," said Jack, hardly knowing how to introduce his business.

" I 'm at leisure now, much as I shall be to-day," said Mr. Peakslow with the air of a man who did not let words interfere with work. " I 've got to grease this wagon, and then harness up and go to haulin'. I have n't had a hoss that would pull his share of a decent load till now. Tend to what you 're about, Zeph ! "

" I have called to say," remarked Jack as calmly as he could, though his heart was beating fast, " that there is a horse in your pasture which belongs to me."

The man straightened his bent back, and looked blackly at the speaker, while the grease dripped from the end of the stick.

" A hoss in my pastur' that belongs to you ! What do ye mean by that ? "

" Perhaps you have n't seen this handbill ? "   And

Jack took the printed description of Snowfoot from
his pocket, unfolded it, and handed it to the astonished Peakslow.

THE AMIABLE MR. PEAKSLOW.

"'Twenty dollars reward,'" he read.   "'Stolen
from the owner — a light, reddish roan hoss — white

forefeet — scar low down on the near side, jest behind the shoulder — smaller scar on the off hip.' What's the meanin' of all this?" he said, glancing at Jack.

"Is n't it plain enough?" replied Jack, quietly standing his ground. "That is the description of the stolen horse; the horse is down in your pasture."

"Do you mean to say *I* 've stole your hoss?" demanded Peakslow, his voice trembling with passion.

"Not by any means. He may have passed through a dozen hands since the thief had him. All I know is, he is in your possession now."

"And what if he is?"

"Why, naturally a man likes to have what is his own, does n't he? Suppose a man steals your horse; you find him after a while in my stable; is he your horse, or mine?"

"But how do I know but this is a conspyracy to cheat me out of a hoss?" retorted Peakslow, looking again at the handbill, with a terrible frown. "It may have all been cut and dried aforehand. You 've your trap sot, and, soon as ever the animal is in my hands, ye spring it. How do I know the hoss is yourn, even if ye have got a description of him? Anybody can make a description of anybody's hoss, and then go and claim him. Besides, how happens it a boy like you owns a hoss, anyway?"

In a few words Jack told his story, accounting at once for his ownership, and for the scars on the horse's side and hip.

"There are two other scars I can show you, under his belly. I did n't mention them in the hand-bill, because they are not noticeable, unless one is looking for them."

"Ye may show me scars all over him, fur 's I know," was Peakslow's reply to this argument. "That may prove that he 's been hurt by suth'n or other, — elephant, or not; but it don't prove you ever owned him."

"I can satisfy you with regard to that," said Jack, confidently. "Do you object to going down with me and looking at him?"

"Not in the least, only wait till I git this wheel on. Ye may go and *see* the hoss in my presence, but ye can't *take* the hoss, without I 'm satisfied you 've the best right to him."

"That 's all I ask, Mr. Peakslow; I want only what belongs to me. If you are a loser, you must look for redress to the man who sold you my property; and he must go back on the next man."

"How 's that?" put in Zeph, grinning over his grease-pot. "Pa thinks he 's got a good deal better hoss than he put away; and you ain't agoin' to crowd him out of a good bargain, I bet!"

"Hold your tongue!" growled Peakslow. "I can fight my own battles, without any of your tongue. I put away a pooty good hoss, and I gin fifteen dollars to boot."

"What man did you trade with?" Jack inquired.

"A truckman in Chicago. He liked my hoss, and

I liked hisn, and we swapped. He wanted twenty dollars, I offered him ten, and we split the difference. He won't want to give me back my hoss and my money, now; and ye can't blame him. And the next man won't want to satisfy *him*. Grant the hoss is stole, for the sake of the argyment," said Peakslow. " I maintain that when an animal that 's been stole, and sold, and traded, finally gits into an honest man's hands, it 's right he should stay there."

" Even if it 's your horse, and the honest man who gets him is your neighbor ?" queried Jack.

" I do'no' — wal — yes !" said Peakslow. " It 's a hard case, but no harder one way than t' other."

" But the law looks at it in only one way," replied Jack. "And with reason. Men must be careful how they deal with thieves or get hold of stolen property. How happens it that you, Mr. Peakslow, did n't know that such a horse had been stolen ? Some of your neighbors knew it very well."

" Some of my neighbors I don't have nothin' to say to," answered Peakslow, gruffly. "If you mean the Bettersons, they 're a pack of thieves and robbers themselves, and I don't swap words with none of 'em, without 't is to tell 'em my mind; that I do, when I have a chance."

" You use pretty strong language when you call them thieves and robbers, Mr. Peakslow."

" Strong or not, it 's the truth. Hain't they cheated me out o' the best part of my farm ? "

" The Bettersons — cheated you !" exclaimed Jack.

They were now on the way to the pasture ; and Peakslow, in a sort of lurid excitement, pointed to the boundary fence.

"My line, by right, runs five or six rod t' other side. I took up my claim here, and Betterson bought hisn, 'fore ever the guv'ment survey run through. That survey fixed my line 'way over yender in their cornfield. And there I claim it belongs, to this day."

"But, Mr. Peakslow, how does it happen that a man like Mr. Betterson has been able to rob a man like *you*, — take a part of your farm before your very eyes ? He is a rather slack, easy man ; while you, if I 'm not greatly mistaken, are in the habit of standing up for your rights."

"I can gin'ly look out for myself," said Peakslow. "And don't suppose that Lord Betterson took me down and put his hands in my pockets, alone."

"Nine men, with masks on," cried Zeph, "come to our house one night, and told pa they 'd jest tear his ruf right down over his head, and drive him out of the county, if he did n't sign a deed givin' Betterson that land."

"Hold your yawp, Zeph !" muttered Peakslow. "I can tell my own story. There was nine of 'em, all armed, and what could I do ?"

"This is a most extraordinary story !" exclaimed Jack. "Did you sign the deed ? "

"I could n't help myself," said Peakslow.

"It seems to me I *would* have helped myself, if

the land was rightfully mine!" cried Jack. "They *might* tear my house down, — they *might* try to drive me out of the county, — I don't believe I would deed away my land, just because they threatened me, and I was afraid."

"It's easy to talk that way," Peakslow replied. "But, come case in hand, — the loaded muzzles in your face, — you'd change your mind."

"Did n't they pay for the land they took?"

"Barely nothin'; jest the guv'ment price; dollar 'n' a quarter an acre. But jest look at that land to-day, — the best in the State, — wuth twenty dollars an acre, if 't is a cent."

"What was Betterson's claim?" Jack asked; "for men don't often do such things without some sort of excuse."

"They hild that though the survey gin me the land, it was some Betterson had supposed belonged to his purchase. Meanwhile he had j'ined a land-claim society, where the members all agreed to stand by one another; and that was the reason o' their takin' sich high-handed measures with me."

Jack was inclined to cross-question Peakslow, and sift a little this astonishing charge against Betterson and the land-claim society. But they had now reached the pasture bars, and the question relating to the ownership of the horse was to be settled.

The Betterson boys were still sitting on the fence, where Jack had left them; but Snowfoot had returned to his grazing.

"Call him," said Jack. "If he does n't come for you, then see if he will come for me."

Peakslow grumblingly declined the test.

"He does n't always come when I call him," said Jack. "I 'll show you what I do then. Here, Lion!"

He took from his pocket an ear of corn he had picked by the way, placed one end of it between the dog's jaws, saying, "Bring Snowfoot, Lion! bring Snowfoot!" and let him through the bars.

Lion trotted into the pasture, trotted straight up to the right horse, coaxed and coquetted with him for a minute, and then trotted back. Snowfoot followed, leering and nipping, and trying to get the ear of corn.

Lion brought the ear to Jack, and Jack gave it to Snowfoot, taking him at the same time by the forelock.

"What do you think of that?" he said, looking round in triumph at Peakslow.

"I don't see as it 's anything to make sich a fuss over," said Peakslow, looking angrily across at the spectators on the boundary fence, as they cheered the success of the manœuvre. "It shows you 've larnt your dog tricks, — nothin' more. 'Most any hoss would foller an ear of corn that way."

"Why did n't your hoss follow it?"

"The dog did n't go for my hoss."

"Why did n't he go for your horse, as soon as for mine?" urged Jack.

H

To which Peakslow could only reply, —

"Ye need n't let down the top bar; ye can't take that hoss through! I traded for him, and paid boot, and you 've got to bring better evidence than your say-so, or a dog's trick, 'fore I give up my claim."

"I 'll bring you evidence," said Jack, turning away in no little impatience and disgust.

He hastened back to Mr. Betterson's house, and was met by the boys as he came into the yard.

"What did I tell you?" said Rufe. "Could n't get him, could you?"

"No, but I will!" replied Jack, untying the horse, which he had left hitched to an oak-tree. "I 'm going for a witness." He backed the wagon around. "Get in, if you like," — to Rufus.

Rufus did like; and the two rode off together, to the great dissatisfaction of Wad and Link, who also wanted to go and see the fun.

CHAPTER XV.

GOING FOR A WITNESS.

"DID Peakslow say anything to you about our folks ? " Rufe asked.

"I rather think he did!" said Jack; and he repeated the story of the land robbery.

Rufe showed his contempt for it by a scornful laugh. "I 'll tell you just what there is in it; and it will show you the sort of man you have to deal with. We have n't an inch of his land. Do you think father is a man to crowd a neighbor ?"

"And a neighbor like Peakslow! That's just what I told him," said Jack.

"You see," said Rufe, "these claims through here were all taken up before the government survey. Most of the settlers were decent men; and they knew that when the survey came to be made, there would be trouble about the boundaries, if they did n't take measures beforehand to prevent it. So they formed a society to protect each other against squatters and claim-jumpers, and particularly to settle disputed boundary questions between themselves. They all signed a paper, agreeing to 'deed and redeed,' — that is, if your land adjoined mine, and the government survey did n't correspond with our lines, but

gave you, for instance, a part of the land I had im-
proved, then you agreed to redeed that part to me,
for the government price; just as I agreed to redeed
to my neighbors what the survey might give me of
their claims."

"I understand," said Jack.

"Well, father and almost everybody in the county
joined the society; but there were some who did n't.
Peakslow was one."

"What were his objections?"

"He could n't give any good ones. All he would
say was, 'I 'll see; I 'll think about it.' He was just
waiting to see if there was any advantage to be
gained over his neighbors by *not* joining with them.
Finally, the survey came through; and the men run
what they called a 'random line,' which everybody
thought, at first, was the true line. According to
that, the survey would have given us a big strip of
Peakslow's farm, including his house and barn. That
frightened him. He came over, and shook his fist in
father's face, and threatened I don't know what, if he
took the land.

"'You really think I ought to redeed to you all
your side of our old line?' says father.

"'Of course I do!' says Peakslow. 'It 's mine;
you never claimed it; and I 'll shoot the fust man
who sets foot on 't, to take it away from me.'

"'Then,' says father, 'why don't you join the society, and sign the agreement to redeed, with the rest
of us? That will save trouble.'

"So Peakslow rushed off in a fearful hurry, and put his name to the paper. Then — what do you think? The surveyors, in a few days, run the correct line, and that gave Peakslow a strip of *our* farm."

"Capital!" laughed Jack.

"It was n't capital for us! He was then, if you will believe it, more excited than when the boot seemed to be on the other leg. He vowed that the random line was a mere pretence to get him to sign the agreement; that it was all a fraud, which he never would submit to; that he would n't redeed, but that he would have what the survey gave him. That's the kind of man he is," added Rufus.

"But he did redeed?"

"Yes, in some such way as he told you. The dispute came before the society for arbitration, and of course the decision was in father's favor. But Peakslow still held out, and talked of shooting and all that sort of thing, till the society got tired of his nonsense. So, one night, nine men did give him a call; they had called on a claim-jumper down the river a few nights before, and made kindling-wood of his shanty; Peakslow knew it, and knew they were not men to be trifled with. They told him that if he expected to live in the county, he must sign the deed. And he signed it. My father was n't one of the men, but Peakslow turned all his spite against him."

"He imagines he has been wronged," said Jack.

"I suppose so, for he is one of that kind who

never can see any side to a quarrel but their own.
The land is growing more valuable every year; he
covets it accordingly, and so the ferment in his mind
is kept up. Of course," Rufe confessed, "we have
done, or neglected to do, a good many things which
have kept adding fuel to the fire; for it's impossible
to live peaceably alongside of such a selfish, passion-
ate, unreasonable neighbor. We boys have taken up
the quarrel, and now I owe that Zeph a cudgelling,
for hurting Cecie."

"How did he hurt her?"

"We had a swing up in the woods. The Peakslows are always interfering in our affairs, and, one
day, when Link and the girls went to swing, they
found a couple of little Peakslows there. Link drove
'em away, and they went off bellowing to their big
brothers. In a little while Zeph came along, when
Cecie happened to be in the swing; and he pushed
her so hard that she fell out."

"I should n't think cudgelling him would give you
much satisfaction," said Jack. "It was a dreadful
thing to happen! But did he intend it?"

"I don't think he is sorry for it. Father went
to see Mr. Peakslow about it; but he got nothing
but abuse from him. What do you think he said?
'The swing,' says he, 'is on a part of the land you
robbed me of; if you had gin me what the guv'-
ment survey did, then your children would n't have
been there, and the thing would n't have occurred.'
That is the man who has got your horse."

Meanwhile, they had driven past Peakslow's house, proceeding down the river road; and now once more Jack reined up before old Wiggett's cabin.

At the sight of the wagon approaching three or four half-naked little barbarians ran into the house, like wild creatures into their hole, giving an alarm which brought out old Wiggett himself, stooping through the low doorway.

"Mr. Wiggett, do you remember me?" said Jack.

"Wal, I reckon!" said the old man, advancing to the wagon, reaching up, and giving Jack's hand a hearty shake. "You're the young chap that found my section corner."

"And do you remember my horse?"

"I 'low I oughter; for your elephant story, and the scars you showed me, was drea'ful curi's. I heard the hoss was stole."

"He *was* stolen. But I have found him; and I want you to go with me and identify him, if you will be so good. Mr. Peakslow has him."

"Peakslow?" said the old man, with a dubious shake of the head. "It's nigh about the easiest thing in the world to git into trouble with Dud Peakslow. I gener'ly go my way, and let Peakslow go hisn, and waste few words on him. But I don't mind gwine with ye, if ye say so. How did Peakslow come by him?"

Jack told the story, whilst driving back to Peakslow's house. There he left Rufus in the wagon, and walked on with Mr. Wiggett into the barnyard.

CHAPTER XVI.

PEAKSLOW GETS A QUIRK IN HIS HEAD.

PEAKSLOW had finished greasing his wheels, and was about harnessing a pair of horses which Zeph held by their halters at the door of a log-stable. One of the horses was Snowfoot.

"Please wait a minute, Mr. Peakslow," said Jack, turning pale at the sight. "I 've brought a witness to prove my property."

Peakslow looked at his neighbor Wiggett, and gave a grunt.

"So you 've come to interfere in this business, hey?"

Mr. Wiggett made no reply, but walked up to Snowfoot, stroked his sides, examined the scars, looked at him before and behind, and nodded slowly several times. Then he spoke.

"I hain't come over to interfere in nobody's business, Mr. Peakslow. But I happen to know this yer young man; and I know this yer hoss. At his request, I 've come over to say so. I could pick out that animal, and sw'ar to him, among ten thousan'."

"What can you swear to?" Peakslow demanded, poising a harness.

"I can sw'ar this is the hoss the young man druv the day he come over to find my section corner."

"That all?"

"Is n't that enough?" said Jack.

"No!" said Peakslow, and threw the rattling harness upon Snowfoot's back. "It don't prove the hoss belonged to you, if ye did drive him. And, even though he did belong to you, it don't prove but what ye sold him arterward, and then pretended he was stole, to cheat some honest man out of his prop'ty. Hurry up, boy! buckle them hames." And he went to throw on the other harness.

Jack stepped in Zeph's way. "This is my horse, and I 've a word to say about buckling those hames."

"Ye mean to hender my work?" roared Peakslow, turning upon him. "Ye mean to git me mad?"

Jack had before been hardly able to speak, for his rising wrath and beating heart; but he was now getting control of himself.

"I don't see the need of anybody's getting mad, Mr. Peakslow. There 's a right and a wrong in this case; and if we both want the right, we shall agree."

"Every man has his own way o' lookin' at the right," said Peakslow, slightly mollified. "The right, to your notion, is that I' shall give ye up the hoss. I 've got possession of the hoss, and I mean to keep possession; and that 's what 's about right, to my notion."

"I want only what is lawfully my own," Jack answered, firmly. "If you want what is n't yours, that 's *not* right, but wrong. There 's such a thing

6

as justice, aside from our personal interest in a matter."

Probably Peakslow had never thought of that.

"Wal, what ye goin' to do about it?" he asked.

"I am going to have my horse," replied Jack. "If you let me take him peaceably, very well. If you compel me to go to law, I shall have him all the same, and you will have the costs to pay."

Peakslow winced. The threat of costs touched him in his tenderest spot.

"How's that?" he anxiously asked.

"I have n't been about the country looking for my horse, without knowing something of the law for the recovery of stolen property," replied Jack. "If I find him in your hands, and you give him up, I 've no action against you. If you hold on to him, I can do one of two things. I can go to a magistrate, and by giving bonds to an amount that will cover all damages to you or anybody else if I fail to make good my claim, get out a *writ of replevin*, and send a sheriff with it to take the horse. Or I can let you keep him, and sue you for damages. In either case, the one who is beaten will have the costs to pay," Jack insisted, turning the screw again where he saw it pinch.

The swarthy brow was covered with perspiration, as Peakslow answered, making a show of bluster, —

"I can fight ye with the law, or any other way, 's long 's you want to fight. I 've got money. Ye can't scare me with your sheriffs and writs. But jest look at it. I'm to be throwed out of a hoss at a busy time o' year. *You* would n't like that, Mr. Wiggett — you nor nobody else."

"No," said Mr. Wiggett, who stood looking on in an impartial way, "it mout n't feel good, I allow. And it don't seem like it would feel much better, to have to stan' by and see a hoss that was stole from me, bein' worked by a neighbor. This yer young man tells a straightfor'ard story, and there's no doubt of its bein' his hoss. You've no doubt on't in your own mind, Dudley Peakslow. If he goes to law, he'll bring his proofs, — he's got friends to back him, — and you'll lose. Then why not come to a right understandin', and save right smart o' trouble and cost. I 'low that 'll be best for both."

"Wal, what's your idee of a right understandin'?" said Peakslow, flushed and troubled, turning to Jack. "*My* hoss is in Chicago — that is, if *this* hoss ain't mine. I might go in and see about gittin' on him back, but I don't want to spend the time, 'thout I can take in a little jag o' stuff; and how can I do that, if you break up my team?"

"Mr. Peakslow," replied Jack, quickly making up his mind what he would do, "while I ask for my rights, I don't wish to put you or any man to an inconvenience." He took Snowfoot by the bridle. "Here is my horse; and, with Mr. Wiggett for a witness, I make you this offer: you may keep him one week, and do any light work with him you please. You may drive him to Chicago, and use him in recovering your horse from the truckman. But mind, you are to be responsible for him, and bring him back with you. Is that a fair proposal?"

"Wal, I do'no' but what 't is; I 'll think on 't."

"I want you to say now, in Mr. Wiggett's presence, whether you accept it."

"I 'll agree to bring him back; but I do'no' 'bout deliverin' on him up to you," said Peakslow.

"Leave it so, then," replied Jack, with a confident smile. "I call you to witness, Mr. Wiggett, that the horse is in my possession now" (he still held Snowfoot by the bridle), "and that I lend him to Mr. Peakslow. Now you can buckle the hames, Zeph," letting go the bridle, and stepping back.

"Gi' me a copy o' that handbill," said Peakslow. "I shall want that, and I ought to have a witness besides, to make the truckman hear to reason."

"If he happens to be an unreasonable man," said Jack, with a smile, "you have the same remedy which I have, — a suit for damages. I don't believe he will wait for that. I 'll see you in one week. Good-day, Mr. Peakslow."

"Looks like you was takin' a big resk, to let him drive the hoss to Chicago," Mr. Wiggett remarked confidentially, following Jack out of the yard.

"I don't see that it is," Jack replied, wiping the sweat from his forehead. "I did n't wish to be hard on him. It does men good, sometimes, to trust them."

"Mabbe. But Dud Peakslow ain't like no other

man ye ever see. He's got some quirk in his head,
or he never'd have agreed to be responsible for the
hoss and bring him back; ye may bet on that. He
means to take some advantage. Now I'm interested
in the case, and I shall hate to see you swindled."

Jack thanked the old man warmly; but he failed
to see what advantage Peakslow could hope to gain.

"I know him a heap better'n you dew," said
Mr. Wiggett. "Now, it struck me, when he said
he might need a witness, I'd offer to go with him
to Chicago. I could help him with the truckman,
and mabbe find out what new trick he's up tew.
Anyhow, I could look arter your hoss a little."

"That would oblige me ever so much!" exclaimed
Jack. "But I see no reason why you should take
that trouble for me."

"I take a notion tew ye, in the fust place. Next
place, I've been gwine to Chicago for the past tew
weeks, but couldn't somehow git started. Now,
banged if I won't go in with Peakslow!"

Having parted with Jack, the old man returned to
propose the arrangement to his neighbor. He was
just in time to hear Peakslow say to his son, —

"I see a twist in this matter 't he don't, shrewd
as he thinks he is. If I lose a good bargain, I'm
bound to make it up 'fore ever this hoss goes out
of my hands. You ag'in, Wiggett?"

It was Mr. Wiggett, who concluded that he was
quite right in saying that Peakslow had a quirk in
his head.

CHAPTER XVII.

VINNIE MAKES A BEGINNING.

VINNIE learned only too soon why Jack had dreaded so much to have her enter the Betterson household; and, in a momentary depression of spirits, she asked herself whether, if she had known all she was undertaking, she would not have shrunk from it.

The sight of the sick ones, the mother enfeebled in mind as well as in body, Lord Betterson pompous and complacent in the midst of so much misery, little Lill alone making headway against a deluge of disorder, — all this filled her with distress and dismay.

She could think of no relief but in action.

"I shall stifle," thought she, "unless I go to work at once, setting things to rights."

And the thought of helping others cheered herself. She needed something from her trunk. That was at the door, just where Jack had left it. She went out, and found that Chokie had changed his mind with regard to digging a well, and was building a pyramid, using the door-yard sand for his material, a shingle for a shovel, and the trunk for a foundation.

"Why, Chokie!" she said; "what are you doing?"

"I makin' a Fourth-of-Duly," replied Chokie, flourishing his shingle. "After I dit it about twice as bid as the house, I doin' to put some powder in it, and tout'th it off."

"O dear!" said Vinnie; "I'm afraid you'll blow my trunk to pieces; and I must have my trunk now!"

"I doin' to blow it to pieces, and you tan't have it," cried Chokie, stoutly.

"But I've something for you in it," said Vinnie, "and we never can get it for you, if you touch off your Fourth-of-July on it."

"O, wal, you may dit it." And he began to shovel the sand off, throwing it into his clothing, into the house, and some into Vinnie's eyes.

Lord Betterson, who was walking leisurely about his castle, now came forward, and, seeing Vinnie in some distress, inquired, in his lofty way, if he could do anything for her.

"If you please," she replied, laughing, as she brushed the sand away from her eyes, "I should like to have this trunk carried in."

Betterson drew himself up with dignified surprise; for he had not meant to proffer any such menial service. Vinnie perceived the little mistake she had made; but she was not so overpoweringly impressed by his nobility as to think that an apology was due. She even permitted herself to be amused; and, retiring behind the sand in her eyes, which she made a great show of winking and laughing away, she waited to see what he would do.

He looked around, and coughed uncomfortably.

"Where are the boys?" he asked. "This — hem — is very awkward. I don't know why the trunk was left here; I directed that it should be taken to Cecie's room." -

Vinnie mischievously resolved that the noble Betterson back should bend beneath that burden.

"It is quite light," she said. "If you want help, I can lift one end of it."

The implication that it was not greatness of character, but weakness of body, which kept him above such service, touched my lord. As she, at the same time, actually laid hold of one handle, he waived her off, with ostentatious gallantry.

"Permit me!" And, with a smile of condescension, which seemed to say, "The Bettersons are not used to this sort of thing; but they can always be polite to the ladies," he took up the trunk by both handles, and went politely *backward* with it into the house, a performance at which Jack would have smiled. I say *performance* advisedly, for Betterson showed by his bearing, lofty and magnificent even under the burden, that this was not an ordinary act of an ordinary man.

Having set down the trunk in its place, he brushed his fingers with a soiled handkerchief, and retired, exceedingly flushed and puffy in his tight stock.

Vinnie thanked him with charming simplicity; while Cecie, on her lounge, laughed slyly, and Mrs. Betterson looked amazed.

"Why, Lavinia! how did you ever dare?"

"Dare what?"

"To ask Mr. Betterson to carry your trunk?"

VINNIE'S STRATAGEM.

"Why not?" said Vinnie, with round eyes.

"A gentleman like him! and a Betterson!" replied Caroline, in a whisper of astonishment and awe.

6 *   I

"Who should have done it?" said Vinnie, trying hard to see the enormity of her offence. "I couldn't very well do it alone; I am sure you couldn't have helped me; and my friend who brought me over, he has done so much for me already that I should have been ashamed to ask him. Besides, he is not here, and I wanted the trunk. Mr. Betterson seems very strong. Has he the rheumatism?"

"O Lavinia! Lavinia!" — and Caroline wrapped her red shawl despairingly about her. "But you will understand Mr. Betterson better by and by. You are quite excusable now. Arthur, dear! what do you want?"

"In her trunt, what she's doin' to dive me, I want it," said the boy, invading the house for that purpose.

"Yes, you shall have it," cried Vinnie, skilfully giving his nose a wipe behind the mother's back (it needed it sadly). "But is your name Arthur? I thought they called you Chokie."

"Chokie is the nickname for Arthur," Lill explained.

Vinnie did not understand how that could be.

"It is the boys' invention; they are full of their nonsense," said Caroline, with a sorrowful head-shake. "It was first Arthur, then Artic, then Artichoke, then Chokie, — you see?"

Vinnie laughed, while her sister went on, in complaining accents, —

"I tell them such things are beneath the dignity of our family; but they will have their fun."

Vinnie took from her trunk a barking dog and a candy meeting-house, which made Chokie forget all about his threatened Fourth-of-July. She also had a pretty worsted scarf of many colors for Lill, and a copy of Mrs. Hemans's Poems — popular in those days — for Cecie.

"For you, sister Caroline," she added, laughing, "I have brought — myself."

"This book is beautiful, and I love poetry so much!" said Cecie, with eyes full of love and gratitude. "But you have brought mother the best present."

"O, you don't know about that!" replied Vinnie.

"Yes, I do," said Cecie, with a smile which seemed to tremble on the verge of tears. And she whispered, as Vinnie bent down and kissed her, "I love you already; we shall all love you so much!"

"Dear Cecie!" murmured Vinnie in the little invalid's ear, "that pays me for coming. I am glad I am here, if only for your sake."

"I dot the bestest pwesents," cried Chokie, sitting on the floor with his treasures. "Don't tome here, Lill; my dod will bite!" He made the little toy squeak violently. "He barks at folks doin' to meetin'. Dim me some pins."

"What do you want of pins?" Vinnie asked, taking some from her dress.

"To make mans and womans doin' to meetin'. One dood bid black pin for the minister," said Chokie.

Vinnie helped him stick up the pins in the floor, and even found the required big black one to head the procession. Then she pointed out the extraordinary fact of the dog being so much larger than the entire congregation; at which even the sad Caroline smiled, over her sick babe. Chokie, however, gloried in the superior size and prowess of the formidable monster.

Lill was delighted with her scarf, — all the more so when she learned that it had been wrought by Vinnie's own hand.

"O Aunt Vinnie!" said Cecie; "will you teach me to do such work? I should enjoy it so much — lying here!"

"With the greatest pleasure, my dear!" exclaimed Vinnie, her heart brimming with hope and joy at sight of the simple happiness her coming had brought.

She then hastened to put on a household dress; while Cecie looked at her book, and Lill sported her scarf, and Chokie earned himself a new nickname, — that of Big-Bellied Ben, — by making a feast of his meeting-house, beginning with the steeple.

CHAPTER XVIII.

VINNIE'S NEW BROOM.

RETURNING from his interview with Mr. Peakslow, Jack drove up on the roadside before the " castle," asked Rufe to hold the horse a minute, and ran to the door to bid Vinnie good by.

" Here, Link!" Rufe called, "stand by this horse!"

" I can't," answered Link from the wood-pile, "I 've got to get some wood, to make a fire, to heat some water, to dip the chickens, to loosen their feathers, and then to cook 'em for dinner."

" Never mind the wood and the chickens and feathers! Come along!"

" I guess I *will* mind, and I guess I *won't* come along, for you, or anybody, for *she* asked me to."

" She ? Who ? "

" Aunt Vinnie; and, I tell you, she 's real slick." And Link slashed away at the wood with an axe; for that was the Betterson style, — to saw and split the sticks only as the immediate necessities of the house required.

Rufe might have hitched the horse, but he was not a fellow to give himself any trouble that could well be avoided; and just then he saw Wad coming out of the yard with two pails.

Wad, being cordially invited to stay and hold the horse, also declined, except on condition that Rufe should himself go at once to the spring for water.

"Seems to me you're in a terrible pucker for water!" said Rufe. "Two pails? what's the row, Wad?" For it was the time-honored custom of the boys to put off going for water as long as human patience could endure without it, and never, except in great emergencies, to take two pails.

"*She* asked me to, and of course I'd go for *her,*" said Wad. "She has gone into that old kitchen, and, I tell you, she'll make things buzz!"

Meanwhile Jack had gone straight to the said kitchen,— much to Mrs. Betterson's dismay,— and found Vinnie in a neat brown dress, with apron on and sleeves pinned up. He thought he had never seen her look so bright and beautiful.

"At work so soon!" he exclaimed.

"The sooner the better," she replied. "Don't look around you; my sister is sick, you know."

"I won't hinder you a minute," Jack said. "I just ran in to tell you the good news about my horse,— though I suppose you've heard that from the boys, —and to say good by,— and one word more!" lowering his voice. "If anything happens,— if it isn't pleasant for you to be here, you know,— there is a home at Mrs. Lanman's; it will be always waiting for you."

"I thank you and Mrs. Lanman very much!" said Vinnie, with a trembling lip. "But I mean to *make* things pleasant here," a smile breaking through the momentary trouble of her face.

Jack declined an urgent invitation to stay and see what sort of a dinner she could get.

"By the way," he whispered, as she followed him to the door, "who carried in that trunk?" When she told him, he was hugely delighted. "You will get along! Here comes Rufe. Rufus, this is your Aunt Vinnie."

Rufus (who had finally got Chokie to hold the horse's halter) blushed to the roots of his hair at meeting his relative, and finding her so very youthful (I think it has already been said that the aunt was younger than the nephew), and altogether so fresh and charming in her apron and pinned-up sleeves.

She smilingly gave him her hand, which he took rather awkwardly, and said, —

"How d' 'e do, Aunt Lavinia. I suppose I must call you *aunt*."

"Call me just Vinnie; the idea of my being *aunt* to young men like you!"

There was a little constraint on both sides, which Link relieved by pushing between them with a big armful of wood.

"Well, good by," said Jack. "She will need a little looking after, Rufus; see that she does n't work too hard."

"*You* are not going to work hard for *us!*" said Rufus, with some feeling, after Jack was gone.

"That depends," Vinnie replied. "*You* can make things easy for me, as I am sure you will."

"Of course; just let me know if they don't go right. Call on Link or Wad for anything; make 'em stand round."

Vinnie smiled at Rufe's willingness to have his brothers brought into the line of discipline.

"They are both helping me now. But I find there are no potatoes in the house, and I've been wondering who would get them. Lill says they are to be dug in the field, and that she digs them sometimes; but that seems too bad!"

"That's when Wad and Link — there's no need of *her* — I don't believe in girls digging potatoes!" Rufe stammered.

"O, but you know," cried Lill, "sometimes we should n't have any potatoes for dinner if I did n't go and dig them! I don't care, only it's such 'hard work!"

Vinnie looked admiringly at the bright, brave little girl. Rufe colored redder than ever, and said, —

"Don't *you*, now, do such a thing! Only let me know in season what's wanted; I'll be after those boys with a sharp stick!"

Vinnie could n't help laughing.

"So, when we're going to want a handful of wood, a pail of water, or a basket of potatoes, I am to go for you, and you will go for the boys, and drive them up with your sharp stick! I don't think I shall like that. Would n't it be better for you to see that there are always potatoes in the bin, and wood in the box, and other things on hand that you know will be needed ?"

It was perhaps quite as much her winning way as the good sense of this appeal which made it irresistible.

"Of course it would be better! I'll get you a basket of potatoes now, and some green corn, and I'll look out for the water and wood."

"O, thank you!" said Vinnie. "That will make things so much easier and pleasanter for all of us!"

The potatoes and corn were got with a cheerful alacrity which quite astonished Rufe's mother and sisters.

The inertia of a large body being thus overcome, that well-known property of matter tended to keep Rufus still in motion; and while Vinnie, with Lill's help, was getting the dinner ready, he might have been seen approaching the wood-pile with an eye to business.

"See here, Wad! This wood is pretty dry now; don't you think it had better be cut up and got in before there comes a rain ?"

"Yes, s'pose 't would be a good idea."

"We ought to be ashamed," Rufe went on, "to have *her* calling for a handful of wood every time it's wanted, or going out to hack a little for herself, if we're not around; for she'll do it."

"I s'pose so," Wad assented. "Why don't you go

to work and cut it up? I'll sit down on a log and
whittle, and keep you company."

"Pshaw! don't talk that way. I'll go to work at
it if you will. Come! Will you saw, or split?"

Wad laughed, and said he would split, — perhaps
because the sawing must be done first.

"This saw is in a frightful condition!" Rufe said,
stopping to breathe after sawing a few sticks.

"So is this axe; look at the edge! It's too dull
even to split with," said Wad. "A small boy might
ride to mill on it without suffering any very great
inconvenience."

"If father would only file and set this saw, I'd
help you grind the axe," said Rufe.

The paternal Betterson was just then returning
from a little walk about his estate. As he approached, hat in hand, wiping his noble forehead,
under the shade of the oaks, Rufe addressed him.

"We've got to have wood in the house; now
she's come, it won't do to get it by little driblets,
and have her waiting for it and worrying about it.
I'll saw it, if you'll only set the saw; you know
how, and I don't; we'll do the hard work if you'll
furnish a little of your skill."

Rufe knew how to appeal to the paternal vanity.
The idea of furnishing, not labor, but skill, flattered
my lord.

"Ah! let me look at the saw. And bring me the
file. And set out the shave-horse. I'll show you
how the thing is done."

When Link, who in the mean while had been dressing the prairie chickens behind the house, came round and saw his pompous papa sitting under an oak-tree, astride the "shave-horse," filing away at the saw held in its clumsy jaws, and Wad turning the grindstone close by, while Rufe held on the axe, he ran into the house laughing.

"Mother! just look out there! Father and Rufe and Wad all at work at once! Guess the world's coming to an end!"

"I hope some of our troubles are coming to an end," sighed poor Mrs. Betterson, who sat nursing her babe with a bottle. "It's all owing to *her*. A new broom sweeps clean. She brings a very good influence; but I can't hope it will last."

"O mother!" said Cecie, from her lounge, "don't say that. I am sure it will last; she is so good! You'll do all you can for her, won't you, Link?"

"I bet!" was Link's laconic response. "If *they* only will, too, for there ain't much fun in doing chores while father and Rufe and Wad are just loafing round."

He hastened to Vinnie with his chickens.

"Just look out there once! All at it! Ain't it fun?"

It was fun to Vinnie, indeed.

CHAPTER XIX.

LINK'S WOOD-PILE.

The dinner, though late that day, was unusually sumptuous, and Betterson and his boys brought to it keen appetites from their work. Vinnie's cooking received merited praise, and the most cordial good-will prevailed. Even little Chokie, soiling face and fingers with a "drum-stick" he was gnawing, lisped out his commendation of the repast.

"I wish Aunt Vinnie would be here forever, and div us dood victuals."

"I second the motion!" cried Link, sucking a "wish-bone," and then setting it astride his nose, —"to dry," as he said.

"One would think we never had anything fit to eat before," said Mrs. Betterson; while my lord looked flushed and frowning over his frayed stock.

"You know, mother," said Lill, "I never could cook prairie chickens. And you have n't been well enough to, since the boys began to shoot them."

"Lincoln," said Mrs. Betterson, "remove that unsightly object from your nose! Have you forgotten your manners?"

"He never had any!" exclaimed Rufe, snatching the wish-bone from its perch.

"Here! give that back! I'm going to keep it, and wish with Cecie bimeby, and we're both going to wish that Aunt Vinnie had come here a year ago — that is — I mean — pshaw!" said Link, whose ideas were getting rather mixed.

Poor Mrs. Betterson complained a great deal to her sister that afternoon of the impossibility of keeping up the style and manners of the family in that new country.

Vinnie — who sat holding the baby by Cecie's lounge — asked why the family had chosen that new country.

"Mr. Betterson had been unfortunate in business at the East, and it was thought best that he should try Illinois," was Caroline's way of stating that after her husband had run through two small fortunes which had fallen to him, and exhausted the patience of relatives upon whom he was constantly calling for help, a wealthy uncle had purchased this farm for him, and placed him on it to be rid of him.

"I should think you might sell the farm and move away," said Vinnie.

"There are certain obstacles," replied Caroline; the said uncle, knowing that Lord could not keep property from flying away, having shrewdly tied this down by means of a mortgage.

"One thing," Caroline continued, "I have always regretted. A considerable sum of money fell to Mr. Betterson after we came here; and he — wisely, we thought at the time, but unfortunately, as it proved — put it into this house. We expected to have a large part of it left; but the cost of building was such that all was absorbed before the house was finished."

Such was Caroline's account of the manner in which the "castle" came to be built. Vinnie was amazed at the foolish vanity and improvidence of the lord of it; but she only said, —

"There seems to be a great deal of unused room in the house; I should think you might let that, and a part of the farm, to another family."

Caroline smiled pityingly.

"Lavinia dear, you don't understand. *We* could never think of taking another family into *our* house, for the sake of *money!* though it might be well to let the farm. Besides, there is really one more in the family than you see. I think I have n't yet spoken to you of Radcliff, — my husband's nephew."

"You mentioned such a person in your letter to me," replied Vinnie.

"Ah, yes; when I was giving some of the reasons why we had never had you come and live with us. Well off as we were at one time, — and are now in prospect, if not in actual appearance, — we could not very well take you as a child into our family, if we took Radcliff. He was early left an orphan, and it was thought best by the connections that he should be brought up by my husband. I assure you, Lavinia, that nobody but a Betterson should ever have been allowed to take your place in *our* family."

Vinnie pictured to herself a youth of precious qualities and great promise, and asked, —

"Where is Radcliff now?"

"He is not with us just at present. He is of age, and his own master; and though we make a home for him, he 's away a good deal."

"What is his business?"

"He has no fixed pursuit. He is, in short, a gentleman at large."

"What supports him?"

"He receives a limited allowance from our relatives on the Betterson side," said Caroline, pleased with the interest her sister seemed to take in the illustrious youth. "He is not so stylish a man as my husband, by any means; my husband is a Betterson of the Bettersons. But Radcliff has *the blood*, and is *very* aristocratic in his tastes."

Caroline enlarged upon this delightful theme, until Cecie (who seemed to weary of it) exclaimed, —

"O mother, do see how Aunt Vinnie soothes the baby!"

Indeed, it seemed as if the puny thing must have felt the flood of warmth and love from Vinnie's heart bathing its little life.

That afternoon Rufe and Wad sawed and split the wood, and Link (with Chokie's powerful assistance) carried it into an unfinished room behind the kitchen, — sometimes called the "back-room," and sometimes the "lumber-room," — and corded it up against the wall. An imposing pile it was, of which the young

architect was justly proud, no such sight ever having
been seen in that house before.

LINK'S WOOD-PILE.

Every ten or fifteen minutes he called Vinnie or
Lill to see how the pile grew ; and at last he insisted
on bringing Cecie, and letting her be astonished.

Cecie was only too glad of any little diversion.

She could walk with a good deal of assistance; Vinnie almost lifted the poor girl in her loving arms; Link supported her on the other side; and so they bore her to the back-room, where she leaned affectionately on Vinnie, while Link stood aside and pointed proudly at his wood-pile.

"We never could get him to bring in a stick of wood before, without teasing or scolding him," said Lill.

"This is different; there's some fun in this," said Link. "Rufe and Wad have been at work like sixty; and we wanted to see how big a pile we could make."

All praised the performance; and Mrs. Betterson so far forgot herself as to say she felt rich now, with so much nice, dry, split wood in the house.

"But what a remark," she added immediately, turning to Vinnie, "for one of *our* family to make!"

"I was never so proud of my brothers!" said Cecie. "If I was only well enough, how I should like to help pile up that wood!"

"Dear Cecie!" cried Vinnie, embracing her, "I wish you *were* well enough! And I hope you will be some time."

The wood was all disposed of that afternoon, and the boys concluded that they had had a pretty good time over it.

"Now we can loaf for a whole week, and make a business of it," said Wad.

"There's one more job that ought to be done,"

7   J

said Rufe. " That potato-patch. We can't keep the
pigs out of it, and it 's time the potatoes were dug."

" I s'pose so," said Wad. " Wish we had a hired
man."

" It is n't much of a job," said Rufe. " And we
don't want to be seen loafing round, now *she* 's here."

" We can go up in the woods and loaf," said Wad.

" Don't talk silly," said Rufe. " Come, I 'll go at
the potatoes to-morrow, if you will. We 'll dig, and
make Link pick 'em up."

" I was going to shoot some more prairie chickens
to-morrow. We 've no other meat for dinner."

" We 'll get father to shoot them. Come, Wad,
what do you say ? "

Wad declined to commit himself to an enterprise
requiring so large an outlay of bone and muscle. All
Rufe could get from him was a promise to " sleep on
the potatoes " and say what he thought of them in
morning.

The next morning accordingly, before the cattle
were turned out of the yard, Rufe said, —

" Shall we yoke up the steers and take the wagon
down into the potato-patch ? We can be as long as
we please filling it."

" Yes, we may as well take it down there and leave
it," Wad assented ; and the steers were yoked accordingly.

Lord Betterson was not surprised to see the wagon
go to the potato-patch, where he thought it might as
well stay during the rest of the season, as anywhere

else. But he *was* surprised afterward to see the three boys — or perhaps we should say four, for Chokie was of the party — start off with their hoes and baskets.

" We are going to let *you* shoot the prairie chickens this forenoon," said Rufe. " You 'll find the gun and ammunition all ready, in the back-room. We are going at the potatoes."

Link went ahead and pulled the tops, and afterward picked up the potatoes, filling the baskets, which his brothers helped him carry off and empty into the wagon-box ; while Chokie dug holes in the black loam to his heart's content.

" We might have had a noble crop here," said Rufe, " if it had n't been for the weeds and pigs. Wad, we must n't let the weeds get the start of us so another year. And we 'll do some repairs on the fences this fall. I 'm ashamed of 'em ! "

CHAPTER XX.

MORE WATER THAN THEY WANTED.

A DOCTOR from North Mills came once a week to visit Cecie and the sick mother and baby. One afternoon he brought in his chaise a saddle and bridle, which he said a young fellow would call for in a day or two. The boys laughed as they put the saddle away; they knew who the young fellow was, and they hoped he would have a chance to use it.

Snowfoot's week was up the next forenoon; and at about ten o'clock Jack, accompanied by Lion, and carrying a double-barrelled fowling-piece, with which he had shot a brace of prairie hens by the way, walked into the Betterson door-yard.

He found the boys at the lower end of the house, with the steers and wagon.

" What 's the news ? " he asked.

" The news with us is, that we 're out of rain-water," Rufe replied.

" I should think so," said Jack, looking into a dry hogshead which stood under the eaves-spout.

" It 's too much of a bother to bring all our water by the pailful. So we are going to fill these things at the river and make the steers haul 'em."

There were three wash-tubs and a barrel, which

the boys were putting up on the bottom boards of the wagon-box, from which the sides had been removed.

Jack was pleased with this appearance of enterprise ; he also noticed with satisfaction that the yard had been cleared up since he last saw it.

He asked about Vinnie, and learned from the looks and answers the boys gave him that she was popular.

"Your saddle came yesterday," said Wad ; "so I s'pose you expect to ride home."

"I feel rather inclined that way. How is our friend Peakslow ? "

"Don't know ; he went to Chicago, and he has n't got back."

"Has n't got back !" said Jack, astonished. "That's mean business ! "

He smothered his vexation, however, and told the boys that he would go with them to the river, after he had spoken with Vinnie.

Entering the house, he was still more surprised at the changes which had taken place since his last visit.

"Her coming has been the greatest blessing !" said Caroline, detaining him in the sitting-room. "We are all better, — the doctor noticed it yesterday ; Cecie and baby and I are all better. Lavinia dear will see you presently ; I think she is just taking some bread out of the oven."

"Let me go into the kitchen — she won't mind me," said Jack.

Vinnie, rosy-red from her baking, met him at the door. He had been very anxious about her since he left her there; but a glance showed him that all had gone well.

"You have survived!" he said.

"Yes, indeed!" she replied. "I told you I would make things pleasant here."

"The boys like you, I see."

"And I like them. They do all they can for me. Rufus even helped me about the washing, — pounded and wrung out the clothes. You must stay to dinner to-day."

"I think I may have to," said Jack; "for my horse has n't come back from Chicago yet, and I don't mean to go home without him."

When he went out he found the boys waiting, and accepted a seat with Wad and Link on a board placed across two of the tubs. Rufe walked by the cattle's horns; while in the third tub sat Chokie.

"You can't sit in that tub going back, you know," said Link.

"Yes, I can! I will!" And Chokie clung fast to the handles.

"O, well, you can if you want to, I suppose!" said Link; "but it will be full of water."

They passed the potato-patch (Jack smiled to see that the potatoes had been dug), crossed a strip of meadow-land below, and then rounded a bend in the river, in the direction of a deep place the boys knew.

"I always hate to ride after oxen, — they go so tormented slow!" said Link. "Why don't somebody invent a wagon to go by steam?"

"Did you ever see a wagon go by water?" Jack asked.

"No, nor anybody else!"

"I have," said Jack. "I know a man in this county who has one."

"What man? I'd go five miles to see one!"

"You can see one without going so far. The man is your father, and this is the wagon. It is going by water now."

"By water — yes! By the river!" said Link, amused and vexed.

"Link," said Jack, "do you remember that little joke of yours about the boys stopping the leak in the boat? Well, we are even now."

Rufe backed the hind-wheels of the wagon into the river, over the deep place, and asked Wad which he would do, — dip the water and pass it up by the pailful, or stay in the wagon and receive it.

"Whoever dips it up has to stand in the river above his knees," said Wad; "and I don't mean to get wet to-day."

"Very well; stay in the wagon, then. You'll get as wet as I shall; for I'm going to pull off my shoes and roll up my trousers. Chokie, you keep in that tub, just where you are, till the tub is wanted. Link, you'd better go into the river with me, and dip the pails, while I pass 'em up to Wad."

"I never can keep my trousers-legs rolled up, and I ain't going to get wet," said Link. Then, whispering to Jack: "There's leeches in this river; they get right into a fellow's flesh and suck his blood like sixty."

Wad proposed to begin with the barrel, and to have Link stand at the end of the wagon, receive the pails, pass them to him, and pass them back to Rufe empty.

"Why not move the barrel to the end of the wagon, and fill it about two thirds full, and then move it back again? I'll help you do that," said Link.

"All right; I'll fill the barrel and one of the tubs; then you shall fill the other two tubs."

Link agreed to this; while Jack smiled to hear so much talk about doing so small a thing.

Rufe went in bare-legged, and stood on the edge of the deep hole, where the water was hardly up to his knees. Much as he disliked, ordinarily, to set about any work, he was strong and active when once roused; and the pails of water went up on the wagon about as fast as Wad cared to take them.

"Hullo! Don't slop so! You're wetting my feet!" cried Wad.

"I can't keep from spilling a drop once in a while. You might have taken off your shoes and rolled up your trousers as I did."

The barrel was soon two thirds full, and Wad called upon Link to help him move it forward. Link left his seat by Jack's side, and walked back to the rear of the wagon. Wad, as we know, was already there. So was the barrel of water, standing just

back of the rear axletree.   So also was a fresh pail
of water, which Rufe had placed at the extreme end,
because Wad was not ready to take it.

At that moment the oxen, hungry for fresh grass,
and having nipped all within reach of their noses,
started up a little.   Jack, thinking to prevent mischief by running to their heads, leaped from the front
of the wagon.,

This abrupt removal of weight from one end, and
large increase of avoirdupois at the other, produced a
natural but very surprising result.   Chokie in his
tub, though at the long end of the beam, so to speak
(the rear axletree being the fulcrum), was not heavy
enough to counterbalance two brothers and a barrel
of water at the short end.

He suddenly felt himself rising in the air, and
sliding with the empty tubs.   His brothers at the
same moment felt themselves sinking and pitching.
There was a chorus of shrieks, as they made a desperate effort to save themselves.   Too late ; the
wagon-bottom reared, and away went barrel, boys,
tubs, everything.

The oxen, starting at the alarm, helped to precipi-
tate the catastrophe.   Fortunately, Jack was at hand
to stop them, or the dismantled wagon might have
gone flying across the lot, even fast enough to suit
Link's notion of speed.

Rufe made one quick effort to prevent the boards
from tipping up, then leaped aside, while the discharged load shot past him.

7 *

Chokie, screaming, held fast to the sides of his tub with both hands. Wad, intending to jump, plunged into the deepest part of the river. Link made a snatch at the barrel, and, playing at leap-frog over it (very unwillingly), went headlong into the deep hole.

Chokie met with a wonderfully good fortune; his tub was launched so neatly, and ballasted so nicely by him sitting in the bottom, that it shipped but a splash of water, and he floated away, unhurt and scarcely wet at all, amidst the general ruin.

The wagon-boards, relieved of their load, tumbled back upon the wheels. To add to the confusion, Lion barked furiously.

Jack, frightened at first, finally began to laugh, when he saw Chokie sailing away, under full scream, and Wad and Link scrambling out of the water.

"So you were the fellows that were not going to get wet!" cried Rufe. "Pick out your barrel and empty tubs, while I catch Chokie!"

The river, even in the deepest place, was not very deep; and Wad and Link came wading out, blowing water from their mouths, flirting water from their hair, and shaking water from their rescued hats, in a way that made Rufe (after he had stranded Chokie in his tub) roll upon the grass in convulsions.

"Laugh, then!" cried Wad in a rage; "I'll give you something to laugh at!" And, catching up a tub partly filled with water, he rushed with it to take wet vengeance on his dry brother.

Before Rufe, helpless with laughter, could move to defend himself, tub, water, and Wad, all together, were upon him,— the tub capsizing over his head and shoulders, Wad tumbling upon the tub, and the water running out in little rivulets below.

Rufe was pretty wet, but still laughing, when he crawled out, like a snail from under his shell, and got upon his feet, clutching the tub to hurl it at Wad, who fled.

"You are the only one who has got any dry fun out of this scrape!" Rufe said, trying to brush the water out of his neck and breast.

His words were addressed to Jack, and they proved more strictly true than he intended; for just then Chokie, trying to get out of his stranded tub, tipped it over, and went out of it, upon his hands and knees, into the river. By the time he was pulled out and set upon dry ground, the boys were all pretty good-natured.

"How about those leeches, Link? Did you find any?" said Jack.

"I'm too dizzy yet, to think about leeches," replied Link. "I turned a somerset out of that wagon so quick, I could see the patch on the seat of my trousers!"

"I thought I was going through to China," said Wad, "and expected, when I came up, to see men with pigtails."

He stood on the edge of the water, holding another tub for Rufe, if he should come too near.

"Quit your nonsense now!" cried Rufe, "and hand up that barrel."

"I 'll quit if you will, — as the poultry-thief said when the old gobbler chased him. 'Quit, quit!' says the turkey. 'Quit your ownself!' says the thief. And I 'm just of his way of thinking," said Wad.

"Well! help me put this wagon into shape," said Rufe. "Then we 'll fill our tubs and barrel without any more fooling."

The wagon-boards were replaced and loaded without any further accident. The well-filled tubs were set one upon another, and Wad stood holding them; while Link, having placed the board seat over the barrel of water, sat upon it. They found it a pretty sloppy ride; but they could laugh defiance at a little water now. Chokie, it need hardly be said, did not ride in a tub of water, but walked between Jack and Rufe beside the oxen.

CHAPTER XXI.

PEAKSLOW SHOWS HIS HAND.

"HULLO!" cried Link from his perch, as the wagon passed the potato-patch, "there comes Peakslow down the road through the woods, — just turning the corner for home!"

Jack started with sudden excitement.

"Can you see his team?"

"Yes; one of the horses looks like yours; and he has an extra horse led behind."

Jack ran up to the road to get a look, and came laughing back to the house, where the boys and their load of water had by that time arrived.

"He is driving my horse, and leading one of his own. I am going to get my bridle, and call on him."

"You'll come back to dinner?" said Rufe.

"Yes, if you'll have my prairie chickens cooked."

And, leaving the boys to astonish the family with their wet clothes, Jack, with the bridle on his arm, walked down the road.

Just as he was entering Peakslow's yard, he met Mr. Wiggett coming out with his arms full of brown-paper parcels.

"Mr. Wiggett! glad to see you!"

"Same to yourself," replied the old man. "Got

my arms full o' this yer stuff, or I'd shake hands. I've a lot more o' comforts for wife and young uns in the wagon; but I thought I'd lug along suthin, or they would n't be glad to see me."

"Is it all right about the horse?"

"I 'low it's all right."

"Is Peakslow up to any trick?"

"Nary, as I kin diskiver; and I pumped him, tew, right smart, a-comin' over the perairie."

"Did he have much trouble getting back his horse?"

"Not sich a dog-goned sight Truckman's a straightfor'ard, honest chap. Says he guv eighty dollars for your hoss; thinks he had him of the thief himself; and 'lows he knows the rascal. He stuck out a little at fust, and you should 'a' heard Peakslow talk tew him! 'T was ekal to gwine to preachin'."

"What did he say?"

"Said none but a fool or a scoundrel would ca'c'late he could hang ontew a piece o' prop'ty that had been stole, or traded for what had been stole. Talked, of course, just t' other way from what he did when he talked to you. Truckman did n't mind his gab, but when he was satisfied the hoss he put away had been stole, he guv up Peakslow's, and the fifteen dollars to boot. Now, how in the name of seven kingdoms Peakslow's gwine to turn it about to make anything more, beats all my understandin'!"

Jack thanked the old man warmly for the interest

he had taken in the affair, and asked how he could pay him for his trouble.

"I have n't looked for no pay," replied the old man. "But one thing I should like to have ye dew for me, if ever ye come my way agin with yer compass. My woman guv me right smart of her jaw for forgittin' it when ye was thar before. She wants a noon-mark on our kitchen floor."

"All right," said Jack. "She shall have it."

The old man went on with his bundles, while Jack entered Peakslow's yard.

Peakslow, who was unharnessing his team, with the help of two stout boys, looked up and said, in a tone which he meant should be friendly, —

"How are ye? On hand, I see," with a grim smile at the bridle.

"I was on hand a little before you were," replied Jack. "Your week was up an hour ago. Though I don't care about that. You 've got your horse, I see."

"That 's the main thing I went for; course I 've got him. Here 's a paper, with the truckman's name wrote on 't; he wants you to come and see him when you go to town, pervided he don't come to see you fust."

· "Did he say anything about a bridle and a blanket that were on the horse when he was stolen ?"

"He 's got 'em," Peakslow coolly replied; "but as no reward was offered for anything but the hoss, I did n't take 'em."

Jack did n't quite see the logic of this remark.

"Never mind; they are trifles," he said. "It's glory enough for one while, to get my horse again. I've a bridle here for him; I'll slip it on, Zeph, if you'll slip yours off."

"You can slip your bridle on that hoss, and take him away, when you've fulfilled the conditions; not before," said Peakslow.

"What conditions? You don't pretend to claim my horse now you've got your own back?"

"I've got a claim on him," Peakslow replied. "Here's your own handbill for it. Twenty Dollars Reward! I've got back your hoss for ye, and I demand the reward."

This, then, after all, was the quirk in Peakslow's head. The boys grinned. Jack was astounded.

"Peakslow," he exclaimed indignantly, "you know that's an absurd claim! You did n't find my horse and deliver him to me; I found him in your hands, and you even refused to give him up! The truck-man has a better claim for the reward than you have, for he had him first; and then I don't see but the thief himself has a prior claim to either."

"You talk like a fool!" said Peakslow.

"You *act* like a fool and a knave!" Jack retorted, in a sudden blaze. "I won't have any more words with you. Sue for the reward, if you think you can get it. I'm just going to take my horse!"

"Not till the reward is paid, if I live!" said Peakslow, his black eyes sparkling. "Zeph, step and hand out the old gun!"

CHAPTER XXII.

THE WOODLAND SPRING.

VERY pale, with the bridle dangling from his arm, and Lion walking dejectedly by his side (the sympathetic dog always knew when his master was in trouble), Jack returned to the "castle."

Lord Betterson, meeting him in the door-yard, touched his hat and bowed.

"Where — is — your — quadruped?" he asked, with a cool, deliberate politeness, which fell upon Jack's mood like drops of water on red-hot steel.

"That villain! he claims the reward for him! But I never 'll pay it in the world!"

Betterson smiled and said, "Ah! Peakslow! Highly characteristic!"

"He threatened to shoot me!"

"Very likely. He has threatened to shoot *me*, on one or two occasions. I said, 'Shoot!'" (Jack wondered whether he said it with that condescending smile and gracious gesture.) "It is n't agreeable to have dealings with a person who talks of shooting his fellow-men; but I imagine there 's no danger, if you keep cool."

"I could n't keep cool," said Jack. "I got as mad as he was. I could have shot *him*."

K

"That, my friend," Lord Betterson replied, with a wave of the hand, "was an error, — quite natural, but still an error.   You stay to dinner ? "

"Thank you, I have promised myself that pleasure."

Jack was ashamed of having given way to his anger; and he determined from that moment, whatever happened, to keep calm.

As he threw his useless bridle down, and left Lion to guard it, he saw Wad starting off with a pail, and asked where he was going.

"For water," said Wad.

"More water ?   I should think you all had enough for one day ! "

"Yes, for the outer man," drawled Wad. "Where 's your horse ? "

"I concluded to let Peakslow keep him a little longer.   He seemed willing to ; and I am not ready to ride home.   May I go with you ? "

"Glad to have ye," said Wad.

They walked a little way along the road toward Peakslow's house, then entered the woodland, descended into a little ravine, and, on the slope beyond, found a spring of running water in the shade of an oak grove.

Jack was not inclined to talk of Snowfoot, but he had a good deal to say about the spring.

"Why, this is charming !   What a clear basin of water !   Is it always running over ? "

"Always, even in the driest season.   We first

noticed that little stream trickling down into the ravine; and that's about all there was to be seen, till Rufe and I hollowed out this basin."

"Why don't you come here with your wagon and tubs, instead of going to the river?"

"There's no good way to get in here with a wagon; and, besides, we can't dip up more than two or three pailfuls at a time, — then we must wait for the spring to fill."

"You could sink a barrel," said Jack, "and always have that full, to start upon. Now dip your pail, and let's see how long it takes for the basin to fill."

The experiment was tried, and Jack grew quite enthusiastic over the result.

"See! how fast the water comes in! I say, Wad, you've got something valuable here."

"Yes," said Wad. "I only wish the house had been built somewhere near. This is part of the land Peakslow pretended to claim. The swing, where Cecie got hurt, is in the grove, just up here."

The place was so cool and pleasant that Jack let Wad return alone with the water, and walked about the spring and the swing, and up into the woods beyond, calming his inward excitement, until dinner-time.

At table he gave a humorous account of his late interview with Peakslow.

"He was so very cordial in his request that I should leave Snowfoot, that I could n't well refuse,

— though I *did* decline to trouble him, till he brought out a double-barrelled argument, — stub twist, percussion lock, — which finally persuaded me. He is one of the most urgent men I ever saw," added Jack, mashing his potato.

Vinnie smiled, while the others laughed; but her eyes were full of anxiety, as they beamed on Jack.

"Isn't it possible," she said, "to meet such arguments with kindness? I didn't think there was a man so bad that he couldn't be influenced by reason and good-will."

"It might rain reasons on Peakslow, forty days and forty nights, — he would shed 'em, as a duck does water," Jack replied. "Isn't it so, Mr. Betterson?"

"I have certainly found him impervious," said my lord.

"I might have stopped to argue with him, and threaten him with the law and costs of court, and perhaps have settled the matter for five or ten dollars. But the truth is," Jack confessed, "I lost patience and temper. I am not going to have any more words with him. Now let's drop Peakslow, and speak of something more important. That spring over in your woods, Mr. Betterson, — I've been looking at it. Is it soft water?" (Jack lifted a glass and sipped it;) "as good for washing as it is for the table?"

"It is excellent water for any purpose," said Mr.

Betterson. "There is only one fault in that spring, — it is too far off."

"We are going to move the house up there, so as to have it handy," said Link.

"That is one of my young friend's jokes," said Jack. "But, seriously, Mr. Betterson, instead of moving the house to the spring, why don't you bring the spring to the house?"

"How do you mean? It does n't seem quite — ah — practicable, to move a spring that way."

"I don't mean the spring itself, of course, but the water. You might have that running, a constant stream, in your kitchen or back-room."

"I apprehend your drift," said Betterson, helping Jack to a piece of prairie chicken. "You mean, bring it in pipes."

"Thank you. Precisely."

"But I apprehend a difficulty; it is not easy to make water run up hill."

Jack smiled, and blushed a little, at Betterson's polite condescension in making this mild objection.

"Water running down hill may force itself up another hill, if confined in pipes, I think you will concede."

"Most assuredly. But it will not rise again higher than its source. And the spring is lower than we are, — lower than our kitchen sink."

"I don't quite see that," replied Jack, with the air of a candid inquirer. "I have been over the ground, and it did n't strike *me* so."

"It certainly looks to be several feet lower," said Betterson; and the boys agreed with him.

"We generally speak of going *down* to the spring," said Rufe. "We go down the road, then down the bank of the ravine, and then a little way up the other bank. I don't know how we can tell just how much lower it is. We can't see the spring from the house."

"If I had my instruments here, I could tell you which is lower, and how much lower, pretty soon. While I am waiting for Snowfoot, (I can't go home, you know, without Snowfoot!) I may, perhaps, do a bit of engineering, as it is."

CHAPTER XXIII.

JACK'S " BIT OF ENGINEERING."

THE boys got around Jack after dinner, and asked him about that bit of engineering.

" In the first place," said Jack, standing outside the door, and looking over toward the spring, hidden by intervening bushes on a ridge, " we must have a water-level, and I think I can make one. Get me a piece of shingle, or any thin strip of wood. And I shall want a pail of water."

A shingle brought, Jack cut it so that it would float freely in the pail; and, having taken two thin strips of equal length from the sides, he set them up near each end, like the masts of a boy's boat.

" Now, this is our level," he said; " and these masts are the sights. To see that they are exact, we will look across them at some object, then turn the level end for end, and look across them again ; if the range is the same both ways, then our sights are right, are they not ? But I see we must lay a couple of sticks across the pail, to hold our level still while we are using it."

The boys were much interested ; and Link said he did n't see what anybody wanted of a better level than that.

"It will do for the use we are going to make of
it," said Jack; "but it might not be quite convenient for field service; you could n't carry a pail

TESTING THE LEVEL.

of water, and a floating shingle with two masts, in
your overcoat-pocket, you know. We 'll aim at a
leg of that grindstone. Go and stick your knife
where I tell you, Link."

Jack soon got his level so that it would stand the test, and called the boys to look.

" Here ! you stand back, Chokie !" cried Link; while Rufe and Wad, one after the other, got down on the ground and sighted across the level at the knife-blade.

" Now," Jack explained, " I am going to set this pail of water in your kitchen window, by the sink. That will be our starting-point. Then I want one of you boys to go, with a long-handled pitchfork, in the direction of the spring, as far as you can and keep the pail in sight ; then set up your fork, and pin a piece of white paper on it just where I tell you. As I raise my hand, you will slide the paper up ; and, as I lower my hand, you will slip it down."

Wad and Link both went with the fork, which they set up on the borders of the woodland, back from the road. Then Wad, wrapping a piece of newspaper about the handle, held it there as high as his ·head, with a good strip of it visible above his hand.

Jack, standing in the kitchen, looked across the sights of his level placed in the open window, and laughed.

" What do you think, Rufe ? Is the paper high enough ? "

" It ought to be a foot or two higher," was Rufe's judgment.

" *I* say *a foot* higher," remarked Lord Betterson, coming up behind.

8

" What do you say, Vinnie ? "

" I think the paper is too high."

" Now look across the level," said Jack.

All were astonished; and Lord Betterson could hardly be convinced that the level was constructed on sound principles. It showed that the top of the paper should be just below Wad's knee.

" Now we will take our level," said Jack, after the paper was pinned in its proper place, " and go forward and make another observation."

He chose a place at the top of the ridge beyond Wad, where, after cutting a few bushes, he was able to look back and see the fork-handle, and also to look forward and see the spring. There he set his pail on the ground, waited for the water to become still, adjusted his level, and caused a second strip of paper to be pinned to the fork-handle, in range with the sights.

The boys then gathered around the fork, while Jack, taking a pocket-rule from his coat, ascertained that the second paper was six feet and an inch above the first.

" Which shows that our level is now six feet and an inch higher than it stood on the kitchen window," said he. " Now let's see how much higher it is than the spring."

Link was already on his hands and knees by the pail, turning the sights in range with the spring on the farther side of the little ravine. He suddenly flapped his arms and crowed.

"No need of setting the fork over there," he said. "The spring is *almost* as high as the pail!"

"Let's be exact," said Jack; and he went himself and thrust the fork, handle downward, into the basin of the spring. "Now, Link, you be the engineer; show your skill; tell me where to fix this paper."

Link was delighted with the important part assigned him.

"Higher!" he commanded, from behind the pail. "Not quite so high. Not quite so low. Now just a millionth part of an inch higher — there!"

"A millionth part of an inch is drawing it rather fine," said Jack, as he pinned the paper.

Afterward, going and looking across the level, he decided that Link had taken a very accurate aim. Then, his pocket-measure being once more applied, the paper was found to be only seven inches higher than the water in the basin.

"Seven inches from six feet one inch, leaves five feet six inches as the height of the spring water above the level of our sights at the kitchen window. Now, I measured, and found they were there thirteen inches higher than the bottom of the sink; which shows that if you carry this water in pipes, you can have your spout, or faucet, thirteen inches higher than the bottom of your sink, and still have a head of water of five feet and six inches, to give you a running stream."

The boys were much astonished, and asked how it happened that they had been so deceived.

"You have unconsciously based all your calculations on the fact that you go *down* to Peakslow's. The road falls a little all the way. But it does n't fall much between your house and the place where you turn into the woodland. There you take a path among the bushes, which really rises all the way, though quite gradually, until you pass the ridge and go down into the ravine. Vinnie has n't been accustomed to talk of going down to the spring, as you have; and so, you see, she was the only one who thought Wad at first placed his paper too high. Perhaps this does n't account for your mistake; but it is the best reason I can give."

"How about the pipes?" Rufe asked.

"You can use pump-logs for pipes."

"But we have no pump-logs!"

"You have enough to reach from here to North Mills and return. They are growing all about you."

"Trees!" said Wad. "They are not pump-logs."

"Pump-logs in the rough," replied Jack. "They only need cutting, boring, and jointing. All pump-logs were once trees. These small-sized oaks are just the thing for the purpose; you have acres of them, and in places the timber needs thinning out. You can use the straight stems for your aqueduct, and the limbs and branches for firewood."

"That's an idea!" said Rufe, rubbing his forehead and walking quickly about. "But how are we going to turn our tree-trunks into pump-logs? We have no tools for boring and jointing."

"No, and it would cost a good deal to get them. You want an iron rod, or auger-shaft, long enough to bore half-way through your longest log; then a bit,—an inch bore would be large enough, but I suppose it would be just as easy, perhaps easier, to . make a two-inch bore,—the auger would be more apt to get clogged and cramped in a smaller hole; then a reamer and a circular joint-plane, to make your joints,—the taper end of one log is to be fitted into the bore of the next, you know. You will also need some apparatus for holding your log and directing the rod, so that you sha' n't bore out, but make your holes meet in the middle, when you bore from both ends; and I don't know what else. I 've watched men boring logs, but I don't remember all the particulars about it."

"You seem to remember a good deal," said Wad. "And I like the idea of a stream from this spring running in our back-room,—think of it, Rufe! But it *can't be did*,—as the elephant said when he tried to climb a tree. No tools, no money to buy or hire 'em, or to hire the work done."

"You boys can do a good deal of the work yourselves," said Jack. "You can cut the logs, and get them all ready for boring. Then you can get the pump-maker at the Mills to come over with his tools and help you bore them by hand; or you can haul your logs to him, and have them bored by machinery,—he has a tread-mill, and a horse to turn it. In either case, I 've no doubt you could pay for his labor by furnishing logs for his pumps."

"I believe we can!" said Rufe, by this time quite warmed up to the subject. "But how about laying the logs ? They have to be put pretty deep into the ground, don't they ?"

"Deep enough so that the water in them won't freeze. A trench four feet deep will answer."

"How wide ?"

"Just wide enough for a man to get into it and lay the logs and drive the joints together. And, by the way, you 'd better be sure that there are no leaks, and that the water comes through all right, before you cover your logs."

"But there 's work in digging such a trench as that!" said Wad, shaking his head.

"So there is work in everything useful that is ever accomplished. Often the more work, the greater the satisfaction in the end. But you boys have got it in you,—I see that; and, let me tell you," said Jack, "if I were you, I would take hold of things on this place in downright earnest, and make a farm and a home to be proud of."

"I never could get in love with work," replied Wad. "I 'm *constitutionally tired*, as the lazy man said. The thought of that trench makes my back ache."

"It won't be such a back-aching job as you suppose. You 've only to take one stroke with a pick or shovel at a time. And as for that constitutional weariness you complain of, now is the time in your lives to get rid of it, — to work it out of your blood, — and lay the foundations of your manhood."

"I must say, you preach pretty well!" observed Wad.

"I'm not much of a preacher," replied Jack; "but I can't help feeling a good deal, and saying just a word, when I see young fellows like you neglecting your opportunities."

"If father and Rad would take hold with us, we would just straighten things," said Rufe.

"Don't wait for your father to set you an example," replied Jack. "I don't know about Rad, though I've heard you speak of him."

"Our cousin, Radcliff," said Rufe. "He's a smart fellow, in his way, but he don't like work any better than we do, and he's off playing the gentleman most of the time."

"Or playing the loafer," said Wad.

"Let him stay away," said Jack. "You'll do better without any gentlemen loafers around."

"Did *you* ever do much hard work?" Wad asked.

"What do you think?" replied Jack, with a smile.

"I think you've seen something of the world."

"Yes, and I've had my way to make in it. I was brought up on the Erie Canal, — a driver, ignorant, ragged, saucy; you wouldn't believe me if I should tell you what a little wretch I was. All the education I have, I have gained by hard study, mostly at odd spells, in the last three years. I had got a chance to work on a farm, and go to school in winter; then I took to surveying, and came out here to be with Mr. Felton. So, you see, I must have done something besides loafing; and if I talk work to you I have earned the right to."

"I say, boys!" cried Link, "le's put this thing through, and have the water running in the house."

"It will do for you to talk," said Wad; "mighty little of the work you 'll do."

"You 'll see, Wad Betterson! Hain't I worked the past week as hard as either of you?"

"This thing is n't to be pitched into in a hurry," said Rufe, more excited than he wished to appear. "We shall have to look it all over, and talk with the pump-maker, and do up some of the farm-work that is behindhand."

"Why don't you take the farm of your father," said Jack, "and see what you can make out of it? I never knew what it was to be really interested in work till I took some land with another boy, and we raised a crop on our own account."

Rufe brightened at the idea; but Wad said he was n't going to be a farmer, anyway.

"What are you going to be?"

"I have n't made up my mind yet."

"Till you do make up your mind, my advice is for you to take hold of what first comes to your hand, do that well, and prepare yourself for something more to your liking."

" I believe that 's good advice," said Rufe. " But it is going to be hard for us to get out of the old ruts."

" I know it; and so much the more credit you will have when you succeed."

Jack moved away.

" Where are you going now ?" Rufe asked.

" To reconnoitre a little, and see what Peakslow has done with my horse. I ride that horse home, you understand !"

8 *   L

CHAPTER XXIV.

PREPARING FOR THE ATTACK.

THE boys showed Jack a way through the timber to a wooded hill opposite Peakslow's house. There Link climbed a tree to take an observation.

OLD WIGGETT.

"I can look right over into his barn-yard," he reported to his companions below. "There's old Wiggett with his ox-cart, unloading something out of Peakslow's wagon; and there's Peakslow with him. Hark!" After a pause, Link laughed and said : "Peakslow's talking loud ; I could hear him say, ' That air hoss,' and ' Not if I live !' Now old Wiggett's hawing his oxen around out of the yard."

" I must head him off and have a word with him," said Jack. And away he dashed through the undergrowth.

Reaching a clump of hazels by the roadside, he waited till the old man and his slow ox-team came along.

"What's the news, Mr. Wiggett?" Jack said, coming out and accosting him.

" Whoa ! hush ! back !" the old man commanded, beating his cattle across the face with a short ox-goad. He shook with laughter as he turned to Jack. " It's dog-gone-ation funny! He had a quirk in his head, arter all. Hankers arter that reward of twenty dollars !"

" What did you say to him ? "

" Told him he had no shadder of a claim, — he might sue ye through all the courts in seven kingdoms, he could n't find a jury to give him the reward for stolen prop'ty found in his hands. He said for that reason he meant to hold ontew the hoss till you 'd agree to suthin."

" Where is the horse now ? "

" In Peakslow's stable. He wants to turn him out to pastur', but he 's afraid you 're hangin' round. He has set his boys to diggin' taters over ag'in Bet-

terson's lot, where they can watch for ye. What he
re'ly wants is, for you to come back and make him
an offer, to settle the hash ; for he 's a little skittish
of your clappin' the law ontew him."

" I wonder he did n't think of that before."

" He did, but he says you 'd showed yerself a kind
of easy, accomodatin' chap, and he 'd no notion o'
your gettin' so blamed riled all of a suddint."

" That shows how much good it does to be easy
with a man like him ! " And Jack, thanking old
Wiggett for his information, disappeared in the woods.

He found the boys waiting for him, and told them
what he had learned. " Now my cue is," said he,
" to make Peakslow think I 've gone home. So I
may as well leave you for the present. Please take
care of my saddle and bridle and gun till I call for
them. Good by. If you *should* happen to come
across the Peakslow boys — you understand ! "

Rufe carelessly returned Jack's good-by. Then,
leaving Wad and Link to go by the way of the spring
and take care of the pail and fork, he walked down
through the woods to the road, where he found Zeph
and his older brother Dud digging potatoes in Peakslow's corner patch.

" Hullo ! " Dud called out, so civilly that Rufe
knew that something was wanted of him.

" Hullo yourself and see how you like it," Rufe
retorted.

" Where 's that fellow that owns the hoss ? "

" How should I know ? "

" He stopped to your house."

" That 's so. But he 's gone now."

" Where ? "

" I don't know. He told us to keep his saddle and bridle and gun till he called for 'em, and went off. You 'll hear from him before many days."

Rufe's tone was defiant; and the young potato-diggers, having, as they supposed, got the information they wanted, suffered their insolence to crop out.

" We ain't afraid of him nor you either," said Zeph, leaning on his hoe.

" Yes, you are afraid of me, too, you young black-guard ! I 'll tie you into a bow-knot and hang you on a tree, if I get hold of you."

" Le's see ye do it ! "

Rufe answered haughtily : " You would n't stand there and sass me, if you did n't have Dud to back you. Just come over the fence once, and leave Dud on the other side ; I 'll pitch you into the middle of next week so quick you 'll be dizzy the rest of your natural life."   And he walked on up the road.

" Here ! come back ! I 'll fight you ! You 're afraid ! " Zeph yelled after him.

" I 'll come round and 'tend to your case pretty soon," Rufe replied. " I 've something of more im-portance to look after just now ; I 've a pig to poke."

Dud went on digging potatoes ; but Zeph presently threw down his hoe and ran to the house. Shortly after, he returned ; and then Jack, who had sat down to rest in a commanding position, on the borders of

the woodland, was pleased to see Peakslow lead Snowfoot down the slope from the barn, and turn him into
the pasture.

Rufe got home some time before his brothers, who
seemed to linger at the spring.

"There they are!" said Lill; "Link with the fork
on his shoulder, and Wad bringing the pail."

Rufe was sitting on the grindstone frame, as they
came into the yard.

"Did you hear me blackguard the Peakslow boys?
They think Jack — Hullo!" Rufe suddenly exclaimed. "I thought you was Wad!"

"I am, for the present," said Jack, laughing under
Wad's hat. "Do you think Peakslow will know me
ten rods off?"

"Not in that hat and coat! Lill and I both took
you for Wad."

"I am all right, then! Where's your father? I
wonder if he would n't like to try my gun."

Lord Betterson now came out of the house, fresh
from his after-dinner nap, and looked a good deal of
polite surprise at seeing Jack in Wad's hat and coat.

"Mr. Betterson," said Jack, "Peakslow thinks I
have gone home, and he has turned Snowfoot out to
grass. Now, if I *should* wish to throw down a corner
of the fence between his pasture and your buckwheat, have you any objection?"

"None whatever," replied my lord, with a flourish,
as if giving Jack the freedom of his acres.

"And perhaps," said Jack, "you would like to go

down to the buckwheat-lot with me and try my gun. I hear you are a crack shot."

"I can't boast much of my marksmanship now-adays; I could fetch down a bird once. Thank you, — I 'll go with pleasure."

"You are not going to get into trouble, Jack?" said Vinnie, with lively concern, seeing him tie the halter to his back.

"O no! Mr. Betterson is going to give me a lesson in shooting on the wing. I 'll take the bridle, so that if Snowfoot should happen to jump the fence when he sees me, I shall be ready for him, you know. Now I wonder if we can take Lion along without his being seen. He is tired of sitting still."

"We can take him to the farther side of the corn-field, easily enough."

"That will answer. Come, Lion!" The dog bounded with joy. "Keep right by my heels now, old fellow, and mind every word I say. Don't be anxious about us, Vinnie. And, Rufe, if you could manage to engage the Peakslow boys in conversation, about the time we are shooting hens pretty near the fence, you might help the sport."

"I 'll follow you along, and branch off toward the potato-patch, and ask Zeph what he meant by offering to fight me," said Rufe.

"I·'m going to get up on the cow-shed, and see the battle," said Link. "On Linden when the sun was low, and the buckwheat-patch was all in blow, — I 'm a poet, you know!"

CHAPTER XXV.

THE BATTLE OF THE BOUNDARY FENCE.

THE little party set off, watched by Vinnie with a good deal of anxiety. The dog was left in the edge of the corn; and Jack, with a good milky ear in his pocket, followed Mr. Betterson into the buckwheat-field.

" There 's Wad and his dad after prairie chickens," said Zeph.

" Yes," said Dud, "and here comes Rufe after you. He 'll give you *Hail Columby* one of these days, when I ain't round."

" I 'll resk him," muttered Zeph.

" Look here, you young scapegrace!" Rufe called from over the fence, "I 've come to take you at your word. Want to fight me, do ye? I 'm ready, if you 're particular about it."

" Come near me, and I 'll sink a stun in your head!" said Zeph, frightened.

" You 've got that phrase from the Wiggett boys," said Rufe. "I 'd fight with something besides borrowed slang, if I was you."

Betterson meanwhile brought down a prairie chicken with a grace of gesture and suddenness of aim which Jack would have greatly admired if he had not had other business on his mind.

The bird fell in the direction of the boundary fence. Jack ran as if to pick it up, at the same time giving a low whistle for his dog. He stooped, and was for a minute hidden by the fence from the Peakslow boys, — if, indeed, Rufe gave them leisure just then to look in that direction.

Darting forward to the fence, Jack took down the top rails of a corner, and made a motion to Lion, who leaped over.

"Catch Snowfoot! catch Snowfoot!" said Jack, quickly placing the ear of corn in the dog's mouth.

The horse was feeding some six rods off, near Peakslow's pair, when the dog, singling him out, ran up and began to coquet with him, flourishing the ear of corn.

The boys were talking so loud, and Jack had let down the rails so gently, and Lion had sped away so silently, that the movement was not observed by the enemy until Snowfoot started for the fence. Even then the excited boys did not see what was going on. But Peakslow did.

If Snowfoot had been in his usual spirits he would have soon been off the Peakslow premises. But his long pull from Chicago had tamed him; and though hunger induced him to follow the ear of corn, it was at a pace which Jack found exasperatingly slow, — especially when he saw Peakslow running to the pasture, gun in hand, and heard him shout, —

"Let that hoss alone! I 'll shoot you, and your dog and hoss too!"

Jack answered by calling, "Co' jock! co' jock! Come, Lion! Come, Snowfoot! Co' jock!"

At the same time Zeph and Dud took the alarm, and ran toward the gap Jack had made, — they on one side of the fence, while Rufe raced with them on the other. Meanwhile Betterson, having coolly reloaded his discharged barrel, walked with his usual quiet, dignified step to the broken fence.

"Better keep this side," he said with deliberate politeness to Jack. "You are on my land; you 've a right here."

"Oh! but that horse never will come!" said Jack. "Co' jock! co' jock!"

"He is all right; keep cool, keep cool!" said Betterson.

On came Peakslow, the inverted prow of his hooked nose cutting the air, — both hands grasping the gun, ready for a shot.

Jack did not heed him. Snatching the corn from Lion's mouth, he held it out to Snowfoot: in a moment Snowfoot was crunching corn and bits, and the bridle was slipping over his ears.

"Head him off, boys!" shouted Peakslow. Then to Jack, "Stop, or I 'll shoot!"

"If there 's any shooting to be done," said Betterson, without for a moment losing his politeness of tone and manner, "I can shoot as quick as any-body; and, by the powers above, I will, if you draw trigger on that boy!"

"Take care of him, — go!" cried Jack, giving

Lion the bridle-rein and Snowfoot a slap. Then confronting Peakslow, " I 've got my horse; I 'm

"STOP, OR I'LL SHOOT!"

on Mr. Betterson's land; what have you to say about it ?"

" I 'll shoot your dog !"

"No, you won't!"   And Jack sprang between the
infuriated man and Lion leading off the horse.

Dud and Zeph were by this time on Betterson's
side of the fence, hurrying to head off Snowfoot.

"Keep out of our buckwheat!" cried Rufe.   "By
George, Zeph, now I 've got you where I want you."

"Help!   Dud, Dud — help!" screamed Zeph.

But Dud had something else to do.   He sprang
to seize Snowfoot's bridle; when Lion, without loos-
ing his hold of it, turned with such fury upon the
intruder, that he recoiled, and, tripping his heels in
the trodden buckwheat, keeled over backward.

Meanwhile Rufe had Zeph down, and was rubbing
the soft black loam of the tilled field very thoroughly
into his features, giving especial attention to his neck
and ears.   Zeph was spitting the soil of the country,
and screaming; and Rufe was saying, —

"Lie still!   I 'll give your face such a scouring as
it has n't had since you was a baby and fell into the
soft-soap barrel!"

Jack backed quietly off, as Peakslow, cocking his
gun, pressed upon him with loud threats and blazing
eyes.   The angry man was striding through the gap,
when Betterson stepped before him, courteous, stately,
with a polite but dangerous smile.

"Have a care, friend Peakslow!" he said.   "If
you come upon my premises with a gun, threatening
to shoot folks, I 'll riddle you with small shot; I 'll
fill you as full of holes as a pepper-box!"

CHAPTER XXVI.

VICTORY.

PEAKSLOW halted in the gap of the fence, his fury cooling before Lord Betterson's steady eyes and quiet threat.

Betterson went on, speaking deliberately, while his poised and ready barrels gave emphasis to his remarks, —

"You 've talked a good deal of shooting, one time and another, friend Peakslow. I think it is about time to have done with that foolishness. Excuse my frankness."

"I 've a right to defend my property and my premises!" said Peakslow, glowing and fuming, but never stepping beyond the gap.

"What property or premises, good neighbor? The horse is this young man's; and nobody has set foot on your land."

"That dog was on my land."

"And so was the horse," put in Jack.

"Take him off, pa! he 's smotherin' on me!" shouted Zeph.

"Your boy is abusin' mine. I 'll take care o' *him!*" And Peakslow set a foot over the two lower rails left in the gap.

"You'd better stay where you are, — accept a friend's disinterested advice," remarked Betterson. "If your boy had been on the right side of the fence, minding his own business, — you will bear with me if I am quite plain in my speech, — my boy would have had no occasion to soil his hands with him."

Peakslow appeared quite cowed by this unexpected show of determination in his easy-going neighbor. He stood astride the rails, just where Betterson had arrested his advance, and contented himself with urging Dud to the rescue of his brother.

"Why do ye stan' there and see Zeph treated that way? Why don't ye pitch in?"

"That's a game two can play at," said Jack. "Hands off, Dud, my boy." And he stood by to see fair play.

"My boy had a right on that land; it's by good rights mine to-day!" exclaimed Peakslow.

"We won't discuss that question; it has been settled once, neighbor," replied Betterson. "Rufus, I think you've done enough for that boy; his face is blacker than I ever saw it, which is saying a good deal. Let him go. Mr. Peakslow," — with a bow of gracious condescension over the frayed stock, — "you are welcome to as much of this disputed territory as you can shake out of that youngster's clothes, — not any more."

"That seems to be a good deal," said Jack, laughing to see Zeph scramble up, gasping, blubbering, flirting soil from his clothes and hair, and clawing it desperately from his besmeared face.

"That's for daring me to fight you," said Rufe, as he let him go. "I'll pay you some other time for what you did to Cecie"; while Zeph went off howling.

"No more, Rufus," said Betterson. "Come and put up this fence."

"I'll do that," said Jack. "I'm bound to leave it as I found it; if Mr. Peakslow will please step either forward or back."

Peakslow concluded to step back; and Jack and Rufe laid up the corner, rail by rail.

"Don't you think you've played me a perty shabby trick?" said Peakslow, glaring at Jack.

"You are hardly the man to speak with a very good grace of *anybody's* shabby tricks," Jack replied, putting up the top rail before the hooked nose.

"I didn't think it of you!" And Peakslow cast longing eyes after the horse.

"You must have forgotten what you thought," said Jack. "You didn't dare turn the horse out till Zeph told you I'd gone home; and it seems you kept pretty close watch of him then."

Peakslow choked back his wrath, and muttered, —

"Ye might 'a' gi'n me suthin for my trouble."

"So I would, willingly, if you had acted decently."

"Gi' me suthin now, and settle it."

"I consider it already settled, — like your land-claim dispute," said Jack. "But no matter; how much do you want? Don't bid too high, you know."

"Gi' me a dollar, anyhow!"

Jack laughed.

"If I should give you enough to pay for the charge in your gun, would n't that satisfy you? Though, as you did n't fire it at me, I don't quite see that I ought to defray the expense of it. Good day, Mr. Peakslow."

Jack went to find the chicken that had been shot; and Peakslow vented his rage upon his neighbor across the fence.

"What a pattern of a man you be! stuck-up, struttin', — a turkey-gobbler kind of man, I call ye. Think I 'm afraid o' yer gun?"

"I have no answer to make to remarks of that nature," said Lord Betterson, retiring from the fence.

"Hain't, hey?" Peakslow roared after him. "Feel above a common man like me, do ye? Guess I pay *my* debts. If I set out to build, guess I look out and not bu'st up 'fore I get my paintin' and plasterin' done. Nothin' to say to me, hey?"

Betterson coolly resumed his slow and stately march across the buckwheat, looking for prairie chickens.

"You puffed-up, pompous, would-be 'ristocrat!" said Peakslow, more and more furious, "where 'd you be if your relations did n't furnish ye money? Poorer 'n ye be now, I guess. What if I should tell ye what yer neighbors say of ye? Guess ye would n't carry yer head so plaguy high!"

Two chickens rose from before Betterson's feet, and flew to right and left. With perfect coolness and precision of aim he fired and brought down one, then turned and dropped the other, with scarce an interval of three seconds between the reports.

"This is a very pretty piece of yours," he observed smilingly, with a stately wave of the hand toward Jack.

"I never saw anything so handsomely done!" exclaimed Jack, bringing the chicken previously shot.

At the same time he could not help glancing with some apprehension at Peakslow, not knowing what that excitable neighbor might do, now that Betterson's two barrels were empty.

"I think I will stay and have one or two more shots," said Betterson. "A very pretty piece indeed!"

The muttering thunder of Peakslow's wrath died away in the distance, as he retired with his forces. Rufe picked up the last two prairie chickens and followed Jack, who ran to overtake the dog and horse.

Lion still held the bridle-rein, letting Snowfoot nip the grass that grew along the borders of the corn, but keeping him from the corn itself. Jack patted and praised the dog, and stroked and caressed the horse, looking him all over to see if he had received any fresh injury.

9   M

Then Rufe joined him; and presently Wad came bounding down the slope from the barn, laughing, carrying Jack's coat; and Link appeared, running and limping, having hurt his ankle in jumping down from the cow-shed. Behind came Chokie, trudging on his short legs, and tumbling and sprawling at every few steps.

The boys were jubilant over the victory, and Jack was the object of loud congratulations; while Lion and Snowfoot formed the centre of the little group.

"Much obliged to you, Wad," said Jack, as they re-exchanged coats and hats. "Thanks to you, I've got my horse again. Thanks to all of you. Boys, I was perfectly astonished at your father's pluck!" And he could not help thinking what a really noble specimen of a man Betterson might have made, if he had not been standing on his dignity and waiting for legacies all his life.

"Not many folks know what sort of a man father is," replied Rufe. "Peakslow would have found out, if he had drawn a bead on you. How quick he stopped, and changed countenance! He can govern his temper when he finds he must; and he can cringe and crawl when he sees it's for his interest. Think of his asking you at last, — after you had got your horse in spite of him, and at the risk of your life, — think of his begging you to give him a dollar!"

Jack said, "Look at that galled spot on Snow-foot's neck! Peakslow has got all he could out of him the past week, — kept him low and worked him

RETURNING IN TRIUMPH. — Page 195.

hard in a cruel collar. Never mind, old Snowfoot! better times have come now, for both of us. Here, Link, you are lame; want a ride?"

Link did want a ride, of course, — who ever saw a boy that did n't? Jack took hold of his foot and helped him mount upon Snowfoot's back; then called to Chokie, who was getting up from his last tumble (with loud lamentations), a few yards off.

"Here, Chokie; don't cry; fun is n't all over yet; you can ride too." Tossing the urchin up, Jack set him behind Link. "Hold on now, Chokie; hug brother tight!"

Both chubby arms reaching half around Link's waist, one chubby cheek pressed close to Link's suspender, and two chubby legs sticking out on Snowfoot's back, Chokie forgot his griefs, and, with the tear-streaks still wet on his cheeks, enjoyed the fearful pleasure of the ride.

Vinnie's bright face watched from the door, the delighted Lill clapped her hands, and Mrs. Betterson and Cecie looked eagerly from the window, as the little procession approached the house, — Lion walking sedately before, then Link and Chokie riding the lost horse, and Jack and Rufe and Wad following with the prairie chickens.

More congratulations. Then Lord Betterson came from the field with another bird. Then Snowfoot was saddled, and Jack, with dog and gun, and two of the prairie chickens, took leave of his friends, and rode home in triumph.

CHAPTER XXVII.

VINNIE IN THE LION'S DEN.

WHEN Link the next morning went to the spring
for water he found that the Peakslow boys (it could
have been nobody else) had, by a dastardly trick,
taken revenge for the defeat of the day before.

Link came limping back (his ankle was still sore)
with an empty pail, and loud complaints of the
enemy.

"They've been and gone and filled the spring with
earth and leaves and sticks, and all sorts of rubbish!
It will take an hour to dig it out, and then all day
for the water to settle and be fit to drink."

"Those dreadful Peakslow boys! what *shall* we
do?" Caroline said despairingly. "No water for
breakfast, and no near neighbors but the Peakslows;
but their well is the last place where we should
think of going for water."

"I'll tell you what *I*'ll do!" said Link. "I'll go
to-night and give 'em such a dose in their well, that
they won't want any water from it for the next two
months! I know where there's a dead rabbit. The
Peakslows don't get the start of us!"

"I don't see but that one of the boys will have to
go to Mr. Wiggett's for water," said poor Caroline,
bemoaning her troubles.

"Rufe and Wad are doing the chores," said Link, "and I'm lame. Besides, you don't catch one of us going to old Wiggett's for water, for we should have to pass Peakslow's house, and it would please 'em too well."

"Let me take the pail; I will get some water," said Vinnie.

"Why, Lavinia dear!" Caroline exclaimed, "what are you thinking of? Where are you going?"

"To Mr. Peakslow's," Vinnie answered with a smile.

"Going into the lion's den! Don't think of such a thing, Lavinia dear!"

"No, by sixty!" cried Link. "I don't want them boys to sass you! I'd rather go a mile in the other direction for water, — bother the lame foot!"

But Vinnie quietly persisted, saying it would do no harm for her to try; and putting on her bonnet, she started off with the empty pail.

I cannot say that she felt no misgivings; but the consciousness of doing a simple and blameless act helped to quiet the beating of her heart as she approached the Peakslow door.

It was open, and she could see the family at breakfast within, while the loud talking prevented her footsteps from being heard.

Besides Dud and Zeph, there were three or four younger children, girls and boys, the youngest of whom — a child with bandaged hands and arms — sat in its father's lap.

Vinnie remembered the swarthy face, bushy beard, and hooked nose; and yet she could hardly believe that this was the same man who once showed her such ruffianly manners on the wharf in Chicago. He was fondling and feeding the child, and talking to it, and drumming on the table with his knife to amuse it and still its complaining cries.

"Surely," thought Vinnie, "there must be some good in a man who shows so much affection even toward his own child." And with growing courage she advanced to the threshold.

Mrs. Peakslow — a much-bent, over-worked woman, with a pinched and peevish face — looked up quickly across the table and stared at the strange visitor. In a moment all eyes were turned upon Vinnie.

"I beg your pardon," she said, pausing at the door. "I wish to get a pail of water. Can I go to your well and help myself?"

The children — and especially Dud and Zeph — looked in astonishment at the bright face and girlish form in the doorway. As Mr. Peakslow turned his face toward her, all the tenderness went out of it.

"What do Betterson's folks send here for water for? And what makes 'em send a gal? Why don't they come themselves?"

"They did not send me," Vinnie answered as pleasantly as she could. "I came of my own accord."

Peakslow wheeled round on his chair.

"Queer sort of folks, they be! An' seems to me you must be queer, to be stoppin' with 'em."

"Mrs. Betterson is my sister," replied Vinnie in a trembling voice. "I came to her because she is sick, and Cecie — because I was needed," she said, avoiding the dangerous ground of Zeph's offence.

"I've nothin' pa'tic'lar ag'in Mis' Betterson as I know on," said Peakslow, "though of course she sides with him ag'in me, an' of course *you* side with *her*."

"I've nothing to do with Mr. Betterson's quarrels," Vinnie answered, drawing back from the door. "Will you kindly permit me to get a pail of water? I am sorry if I give you any trouble."

"No trouble; water's cheap," said Peakslow. "But why don't they have a well o' their own, 'ste'd o' dependin' on their neighbors? What makes 'em so plaguy shif'less?"

"They have a well, but it is dry this summer, and —"

"Dry every summer, ain't it? What a way to dig a well that was!"

"They have a very good spring," Vinnie said, "but something happened to it last night." At which Dud and Zeph giggled and looked sheepish.

"What happened to the spring?"

"Somebody put rubbish into it."

"Who done it, did you hear 'em say?"

"I don't know who did it; and I should be sorry to accuse any person of such an act," Vinnie answered with firm but serene dignity.

The boys looked more sheepish and giggled less.

"I know who put stuff in the spring," spoke up a little one, proud of being able to convey useful information; "Dud and Zeph —"

But at that moment Dud's hand stopped the prattler's mouth.

"I don't believe my boys have done anything of the kind," said Peakslow; "though 't would n't be strange if they did. See how that great lubberly Rufe treated our Zeph yist'day! rubbed the dirt into his skin so 't he hain't got it washed out yit."

"I am sorry for these misunderstandings," said Vinnie, turning to Mrs. Peakslow with an appealing look. "I wish you and my sister knew each other better. You have a sick child, too, I see."

"'T ain't sick, 'xac'ly," replied the mother in a peevish, snarling tone. "Pulled over the teapot, and got hands and arms scalt."

"O, poor little thing!" Vinnie exclaimed. "What have you done for it?"

"Hain't done nothin' much, only wrapped up the blistered places in Injin meal; that 's coolin'."

"No doubt; but I 've some salve, the best thing in the world for burns. I wish you would let me bring you some."

"I guess Bubby 'll git along 'thout no help from outside," said Peakslow, his ill-natured growl softened by a feeling of tenderness for the child which just then came over him. "He 's weathered the wust on 't."

But Bubby's fretful cries told that what was left was bad enough.

"I will bring you the salve," said Vinnie, "and I hope you will try it; it is so hard to see these little ones suffer."

She was retiring, when Peakslow called after her, —

"Goin' 'ithout the water?"

"I — thought — you had not told me I could have it."

"Have it! of course you can have it; I would n't refuse nobody a pail o' water. Ye see where the well is?"

"O yes; thank you." And Vinnie hastened to the curb.

"She can't draw it," snickered Zeph. "Handle's broke; and the crank 'll slip out of her hands and knock her to Jericho, if she don't look out."

"Seems to be a perty spoken gal," said Peakslow, turning to finish his breakfast. "I 've nothin' ag'in *her*. You 've finished your breakfast; better go out, Dudley, and tell her to look out about the crank."

With mixed emotions in his soul, Dud went; his countenance enlivened at one and the same time with a blush of boyish bashfulness and a malicious grin. As he drew near, and saw Vinnie embarrassed with the windlass, which seemed determined to let the bucket down too fast (as if animated with a genuine Peakslow spite toward her), the grin predominated; but when she turned upon him a troubled,

9 *

smiling face, the grin subsided, and the blush became a general conflagration, extending to the tips of his ears.

"How does 't go ? "

"It 's inclined to go altogether too fast," said Vinnie, stopping the windlass ; "and it hurts my hands."

"Le' me show ye."

And Dud, taking her place by the curb, let the windlass revolve with moderated velocity under the pressure of his rough palms, until the bucket struck the water. Then, drawing it up, he filled her pail.

The grin had by this time faded quite out of his countenance; and when she thanked him sweetly and sincerely for helping her, the blush became a blush of pleasure.

"It is more than I can carry," she said.   "I shall have to pour out some."

Thereupon Dud Peakslow astonished himself by an extraordinary act of gallantry.

"I 'll carry it for ye as fur as the road ; I 'd carry it all the way, if 't was anywhere else."   And he actually took up the pail.

"You seem to have a very bad opinion of my relations," Vinnie said.

"Good reason !   They hate us, too ! "

"And think *they* have good reason.   But I 'm sure you are not so bad as they believe ; and *you* may possibly be mistaken about *them*.   Let me take the pail now.   You are very kind."

Dud gave up the pail with reluctance, and gazed

after her up the road, his stupid mouth ajar with an expression of wistful wonder and pleasure.

"Hurry now and git up the team, Dud!" his father called from the door. "What ye stan'in' there for? Did n't ye never see a gal afore?"

When Vinnie reached home with her pail of water, all gathered around, eager to hear her adventure.

"The lions were not very savage, after all," she said, laughing.

CHAPTER XXVIII.

AN "EXTRAORDINARY" GIRL.

AFTER breakfast Vinnie left Lill to "do the dishes," and went with her box of salve to fulfil her promise to Mrs. Peakslow. Dud and Zeph were off at work with their father; and she was glad to find the mother alone with the younger children.

"Oh! you ag'in?" said Mrs. Peakslow, by the chimney, looking up from a skillet she was stooping over and scraping. "Ye need n't 'a' took the trouble. Guess Bubby's burns 'll git along."

But Vinnie was not to be rebuffed.

"I have brought some linen rags to spread the salve on. Will you let me do it myself? I wish you would; the poor thing is suffering so."

And Vinnie knelt down beside the girl who was holding Bubby in her arms.

"Is 't any o' the Betterson folks's sa'v'?" Mrs. Peakslow inquired, scraping away at her skillet.

"No; it is some I brought from the East with me, thinking I should find a use for it in my sister's family; it is good for various things."

"Better keep it for her family!" snarled Mrs. Peakslow. Scrape, scrape.

"There 's plenty and to spare," said Vinnie, unroll-

ing her rags. "And my sister will be only too glad
if it can be of any service to you."

"Think so?" Mrs. Peakslow stopped her scraping and scowled at Vinnie. "Her folks hain't never
showed us none too much good-will."

"They have never known you,— you have never
understood each other," said Vinnie. "It is too bad
that the troubles between the men should prevent
you and her from being on neighborly terms. Can I
use a corner of this table to spread the salve? And
can I see the little thing's burns, so as to shape the
plasters to cover them?"

"He tol' me not to use the sa'v', if ye brought
it," said Mrs. Peakslow doubtfully, laying down the
skillet.

"When he sees the good effect of it I am sure he
won't complain; he is too fond of his little boy," said
Vinnie, placing rags and salve on the table. "Will
you let me take a case-knife and a pair of scissors?"

"Got rags enough of my own. Need n't trouble
yourself to cut and spread plasters. *Try* the sa'v', 'f
ye say so."

Vinnie did say so, and dressed Bubby's burns with
her own hands, doing the work so deftly and ten-
derly, talking now to the child, now to the mother,
who had taken him into her lap, and showing in
every look and tone so cheerful and sweet a spirit
that poor Mrs. Peakslow's peevish heart warmed and
softened toward her.

"I do declare," she said, as the outer bandages

were going on, "Bubby feels comforted a'ready.
Must be dreffle good sa'v'! *Much* obleeged to ye,
I'm sure. How *is* yer sister?"

"Much better than she was; and the baby is better too. Indeed," said Vinnie, "I think the baby
will get well as soon as the mother does."

"And Cecie — how's Cecie?" Mrs. Peakslow tim-
idly asked.

"O, Cecie is in very good spirits! She is the most
gentle, patient, beautiful girl you ever saw! She
never complains; and she is always so grateful for
any little thing that is done for her!"

"S'pose the folks feel hard to our Zeph; don't
they?"

"I believe the boys do, and you can hardly wonder
at it, Mrs. Peakslow," said Vinnie; "their own dear
sister! crippled for life, perhaps. But Cecie won't
allow that your son *meant* to hurt her; she always
takes his part when the subject is brought up."

"Does she?" exclaimed Mrs. Peakslow, surprised
into sudden tears. "I wouldn't 'a' believed that!
Must *be* she's a good gal. Truth is, Zeph hadn't no
notion o' hurtin' on her. It's re'ly troubled me, —
it's troubled all on us, though I don't s'pose her
folks'll believe it."

And Mrs. Peakslow, not finding it convenient to
get at her apron, with Bubby in her lap, wiped her
eyes with a remnant of Vinnie's rags.

"Isn't it too sad that this quarrel is kept up?"
said Vinnie.

"O dear me! nobody knows," said Mrs. Peakslow, in a quavering voice, "what a life it is! Our folks is *some* to blame, I s'pose. But the Bettersons have been *so* aggravatin'! Though I 've nothin' ag'in the gals. They 're as perty gals as I 'd ask to have play with my children. My children is sufferin' for mates. I want society, too, for it 's a dreffle life, — a dreffle life!" And the quavering voice broke into sobs.

Vinnie was surprised and pained at this outburst, and hardly knew what reply to make.

"Lyddy, wipe them dishes!" Mrs. Peakslow went on again, sopping her eyes with the remnant of rags. "Lecty Ann! here, take Bubby. Scuse me, miss; I d'n' know what sot me goin' this way; but my heart 's been shet up so long; I 've *so* wanted sympathy!" And now the apron did service in place of the rags.

"Yes, I know," said Vinnie. "This is a lonesome country, unless you have friends around you. There seem to be a few nice people here, — people from the East; you are from the East, I suppose?"

"O yes; but *he* ain't a very social man, an' he 's dreffle sot in his way. He don't go out nowheres, 'thout he has business, an' he don't think there 's any need of a woman's goin' out. So there it is. The Wiggetts, our neighbors on one side, ain't our kind o' people; then there 's the Bettersons on t' other side. An' there 's allus so many things a wife has to put up with, an' hold her tongue. O dear! O dear! Keep to your work, gals! hear?"

There was something almost comical in this sharp and shrill winding-up of the good woman's pathetic discourse; but Vinnie never felt less like laughing.

"I am glad you can speak freely to me," she said. "I'll come and see you again, if you will let me; and I want you some time to come and see my sister."

"I d'n' know! I d'n' know!" said Mrs. Peakslow, still weeping. "*You* may come *here*, — like to have ye, — only it'll be jest as well if you time your visits when me an' the gals is alone; you know what men-folks be."

"You are really an extraordinary girl, Lavinia dear!" Caroline said, when Vinnie went home and told her story. "Did you know it?"

Vinnie laughed.

"Why, no; I never thought of such a thing; what I do comes so very natural."

"Extraordinary!" Caroline repeated, regarding her admiringly. "I'm proud of such a sister. I always told Mr. Betterson there was good blood on our side too. I wonder what Radcliff would think of you."

Vinnie sincerely believed that so fine a young gentleman would not think anything of her at all, but feared it might seem like affectation in he to say so.

"And I wonder," Caroline continued, with the usual simper which her favorite theme inspired, "what you would think of Radcliff. Ah, Lavinia dear! it is a comfort for me to reflect that it was a Betterson — nobody less than a thoroughbred Betterson — who took the place in our family which you would otherwise have filled."

Evidently Caroline's conscience was not quite easy on the subject of her early neglect of so "extraordinary" a sister; for she often alluded to it in this way. Vinnie now begged her not to mention it again.

"And you really cherish no hard feelings ? "

" None whatever."

" You are *very* good. And pretty ; did you know it ? Quite pretty."

Vinnie laughed again.

" Mrs. Presbit brought me up to the wholesome belief that I was quite plain."

" That was to prevent you from becoming vain. Vanity, you know," said Caroline, with her most exquisite simper, " spoils so many girls ! I'm thankful it does n't run in *our* family ! But did n't your glass undeceive you ? "

" On the contrary, I used to look in it and say to myself, 'It is a very *common* face ; I *wish* it was pretty, but Aunt Presbit is right; I'm a homely little thing !' "

" And you felt bad ? "

" I never mourned over it; though, of course, I should have much preferred to be handsome.".

" And has n't anybody ever told you you *were* handsome ? "

Vinnie blushed.

" Of course I've heard a good deal of nonsense talked now and then."

N

"Lavinia dear, you *are* extraordinary.   And handsome, though not in the usual sense of the word.
Your face *is* rather common, in repose, but it lights
up wonderfully.   And, after all, I don't know that
it is so much your face, as the expression you throw
into it, that is so enchanting.   What *would* Radcliff
Betterson say to you, I wonder?"

CHAPTER XXIX.

ANOTHER HUNT, AND HOW IT ENDED.

JACK had one day been surveying a piece of land a few miles east of Long Woods. It was not very late in the afternoon when he finished his work ; and he found that, by going a little out of his way and driving rather fast, he could, before night, make Vinnie and her friends a call, and perhaps give Mrs. Wiggett the promised noon-mark on her kitchen floor.

Leaving in due time the more travelled thoroughfare, he turned off upon the neighborhood road, which he knew passed through the woods and struck the river road near Betterson's house. Away on his left lay the rolling prairie, over a crest of which he, on a memorable occasion, saw Snowfoot disappear with his strange rider; and he was fast approaching the scene of his famous deer-hunt.

Jack had his gun with him ; and, though he did not stop to give much attention to the prairie hens which now and then ran skulkingly across the track, or flew up from beside his buggy-wheels, he could not help looking for larger game.

"I'd like to see another doe and fawn feeding off on the prairie there," thought he. "Wonder if I could find some obliging young man to drive them in!"

He whipped up Snowfoot, and presently, riding over a swell of land, discovered a stranger walking on before him in the road.

"No deer or fawn," thought he; "but there's possibly an obliging young man."

As he drove on, fast overtaking the pedestrian, Jack was very much struck by his appearance. He was a slender person; he walked at a loitering pace; and he carried his coat on his arm. There was something also in the jaunty carriage of the head, and in the easy slouch of the hat-brim, which startled Jack.

"I vow, it's my obliging young man himself!" he muttered through his teeth, — "or a vision of him!"

Just then the stranger, hearing the sound of wheels, cast a quick glance over his shoulder. It was the same face, and Jack could almost have taken his oath to the quid in the cheek.

He was greatly astonished and excited. It seemed more like a dream than anything else, that he should again meet with the person who had given him so much trouble, so near the place where he had seen him first, in precisely similar hat and soiled shirt-sleeves, and carrying (to all appearances) the same coat on his arm!

The stranger gave no sign of the recognition being mutual, but stepped off upon the roadside to let the buggy pass.

"How are you?" said Jack, coming up to him, and drawing rein; while Lion snuffed suspiciously at the rogue's heels.

"All right, stranger; how are you yourself?"   And a pair of reckless dark eyes flashed saucily up at Jack.

"Better than I was that night after you ran off with my horse!" Jack replied.

"Glad you're improving. Wife on the mending hand? And how are the little daisies? Which is the road to Halleluia Corners? I branch off here; good day, fair stranger."

These words were rattled off with great volubility, which seemed all the greater because of their surprising irrelevancy; while the head, thrown gayly to one side, balanced the quid in the bulged cheek.

Before Jack could answer, the youth with a wild laugh struck off from the road, and began to walk fast toward the woodland.   Jack called after him,—

"Hold on! I want to speak with you!"

"Speak quick, then; I'm bound for the Kingdom, — will you go to glory with me?" the rogue shouted back over his shoulder, with a defiant grin, never slacking his pace.

Jack gave Snowfoot a touch of the whip, reined out of the track, and drove after him.

The fellow at the same time quickened his step to a run, and before he could be overtaken he had come to rough ground, where fast driving was dangerous.

Jack pulled up unwillingly, revolving rapidly in

his mind what he should do. Though he had recovered his horse, he felt the strongest desire to have the thief taken and punished. Moreover, he had lately seen the truckman to whom the stolen animal was sold, and had promised to do what he could to help him obtain justice.

He might have levelled his gun and threatened to shoot the fugitive ; but he would not have felt justified in carrying out such a threat, and recent experience had disgusted him with the shooting business.

He would have jumped from the wagon, and followed on foot ; but, though a good runner, he was convinced that his heels were no match for the stranger's. There was then but one thing to do.

" Stop, or I 'll let the dog take you ! " Jack yelled.

For reply, the fugitive threw up his hand over his shoulder, with fingers spread and thumb pointing toward the mid-region of countenance occupied by the nose ; which did not, however, take the trouble to turn and make itself visible.

Lion was already eager for the chase ; and Jack had only to give him a signal.

"Take care of him, Lion ! " And away sped the dog.

Fleet of foot as the fellow was, and though he now strained every nerve to get away, the distance between him and the dog rapidly diminished ; and a hurried glance behind showed him the swift, black, powerful animal, coming with terrible bounds, and never a bark, hard at his heels.

The thickets were near, — could he reach them before the dog reached him? Would they afford him a refuge or a cudgel? He threw out his quid, and *leaned.*

Jack drove after as fast as he could, in order to prevent mortal mischief when Lion should· bring down his game; for the dog, when too much in earnest with a foe, had an overmastering instinct for searching out the windpipe and jugular vein.

The rogue had reached the edge of the woods, when he found himself so closely pursued that he seemed to have no resource but to turn and dash his coat into the dog's face. That gave him an instant's reprieve; then Lion was upon him again; and he had just time to leap to the low limb of a scraggy oak-tree, and swing his lower limbs free from the ground, when the fierce eyes and red tongue were upon the spot.

Lion gave one leap, but missed his mark; the trap-like jaws snapping together with a sound which could not have been very agreeable to the youth whose dangling legs had been actually grazed by the passing muzzle.

With a wistful, whining yelp, Lion gave another upward spring; and this time his fangs closed upon something — only cloth, fortunately; but as the thief clambered up out of their range, it was with a very good chance for a future patch upon the leg of his trousers.

Leaping from his wagon, Jack rushed to the tree,

and found his obliging young man perched comfortably in it, with one leg over a limb; while Lion,

THE END OF THE CHASE.

below, made up for his long silence by uttering fran-
tic barks.

"What are you up there for?" said Jack.

"To take an observation," the fellow replied, out of breath, but still cheerful. "First-rate view of the country up here. I fancy I see a doe and a fawn off on the prairie; would n't you like a shot at 'em ? "

"I 've other game to look after just now !" Jack replied.

"Better look out for your horse; he 's running away !"

"My horse is n't in the habit of running away without help. Will you come down?"

"I was just going to invite you to come up. I 'll share my lodgings with you, — give you an upper berth. A very good tavern; rooms airy, fine prospect; though the table don't seem to be very well supplied, and I can't say I fancy the entrance. 'Sich gittin' up stairs I never did see !' "

Jack checked this flow of nonsense by shouting, "Will you come down, or not ?"

"Suppose not ?" said the fellow.

"Then I leave the dog to guard the door of your tavern, and go for a warrant and a constable, to bring you down."

"What would you have me come down for ? You seem to be very pressing in your attentions to a stranger !"

"Don't say stranger, — you who drove the deer in for me ! I am anxious to pay you for that kindness. I want you to ride with me."

"Why did n't you say so before ?" cried the rogue,

10

rolling a fresh quid in his cheek. "I always ride when you ask me to, don't I? Say, did you ever know me to refuse when you offered me a ride? Which way are you going?"

"Down through the woods," said Jack, amused, in spite of himself, at the scamp's reckless gayety.

"Why, that's just the way I am going! Why did n't you mention it? I never should have put up at this tavern if I had thought a friend would come along and give me a lift in his carriage. Please relieve the guard, and I'll descend."

The dog was driven off, and the youth dropped from the branches to the ground.

"Pick up your coat," said Jack, "and do pretty much as I tell you now, or there'll be trouble. None of your tricks this time!"

He held the reins and the gun while he made the fellow get into the buggy; then took his seat, with the prisoner on his left and the gun on his right, drove on to the travelled track, and turned into the woods; the vigilant Lion walking close by the wheel.

CHAPTER XXX.

JACK'S PRISONER.

FOR a second time Jack now travelled that wood, land road under odd circumstances; the first occasion being that on which he himself had pulled in the shafts, while Link pushed behind. He laughed as he thought of that adventure, of which the present seemed a fitting sequel. Before, he had been obliged to go home without his horse; what a triumph it would now be to carry home the thief! But to do this, great care and vigilance would be necessary; and he calculated all the chances, and resolved just what he would do, should his captive attempt to escape. The rogue, on the contrary, appeared contented with his lot.

"Young man," said he, "I can't call your name, but let me say you improve upon acquaintance. This is galorious! better by a long chalk than a horseback gallop without a saddle. I suppose you will call for me with a barouche next time!"

"At all events, I may help you to free lodgings,— not up in a tree, either!" Jack said, as he touched up Snowfoot.

He had, of course, abandoned the idea of giving Mrs. Wiggett her noon-mark that day. But he could not think of passing the " castle " without stopping at the door.

" What will Vinnie say ? " thought he, with a thrill of anticipation. And it must be confessed that he felt no little pride at the prospect of showing his prisoner to Lord Betterson and the boys.

Descending the long declivity, the fellow was strangely silent, for one so rattle-brained, until the " castle " appeared in sight through an opening of the woods. " He 's plotting mischief," Jack thought. And when suddenly the rogue made a movement with his arms, Jack started, ready for a grapple.

" Don't be excited ; I 'm only putting on my coat."

" All right," said Jack ; and the garment was put on. " Anything else I can do for you ? "

" I 'm dying with thirst ; they had nothing to drink at that tavern where you found me."

" May be we can get some water at this house," Jack said.

" Are you acquainted here ? " the prisoner inquired, with a curious, sober face.

" Yes, well enough to ask for a glass of water." And Jack drove into the yard.

The rogue kept on his sober face, but seemed to be laughing prodigiously inside.

As Jack reined up to the door, Lill came out, clapped her hands with sudden surprise, and screamed, " O mother ! " Then Vinnie appeared, her face radiant on seeing Jack, but changing suddenly at sight of his companion. Mrs. Betterson followed, and, perceiving the faces in the buggy, uttered a cry, tottered, and clung to Vinnie's shoulder.

Link at the same time ran out from behind the house, dropped a dirty stick, wiped his hands on his trousers, and shouted, "Hullo! by sixty! ye don't say so!" while Rufe and Wad came rushing up from the barn. Jack had rather expected to produce a sensation, — not, however, until he should fairly have shown his prisoner; and this premature commotion puzzled him.

The rogue's suppressed laughter was now bubbling freely; a frothy and reckless sort of mirth, without much body of joy to it.

".How are ye all?" he cried. "Don't faint at sight of me, Aunt Carrie. This is an unexpected pleasure!" and he bowed gayly to Vinnie.

"O Radcliff! you again? and in *this* style!" said poor Caroline. "Where *did* you come from?"

"From up a tree, at last accounts. Hullo, boys! I'd come down on my trotters, and hug you all round, but my friend here would be jealous."

Jack was confounded.

"Is *this* your Cousin Rad?" he cried, as the boys crowded near. "I'm sorry to know it, for he's the fellow who ran off with my horse. Where did *you* ever see him before, Vinnie?"

"He is the one I told you about, — in Chicago," said Viunie, astonished to find her waggish acquaintance, the elegant Radcliff Betterson, and this captive vagabond, the same person.

CHAPTER XXXI.

RADCLIFF.

LORD BETTERSON now came out of the house, calm and stately, but with something of the look in his eye, as he turned it upon his nephew, which Jack had observed when it menaced Peakslow at the gap of the fence.

"Ah, Radcliff! you have returned? Why don't you alight?" And he touched his hat to Jack.

"Your nephew may tell you the reason, if he will," Jack replied.

"The long and the short of it is this," said Radcliff, betraying a good deal of trouble, under all his assumed carelessness: "When I was on my way home, a few weeks ago, this young man asked me to drive in some deer for him. He gave me his horse to ride. I made a mistake, and rode him too far."

"You, Radcliff!" said Lord Betterson, sternly; while Mrs. Betterson went into hysterics on Vinnie's shoulder, and was taken into the house.

"We thought of Rad when you described him," Rufe said to Jack. "But we could n't believe he would do such a thing."

"'T was the most natural thing in the world," Rad

JACK AND HIS JOLLY PRISONER — Page 222.

explained. "I was coming home because I was hard up. I did n't steal the horse, — he was put into my hands; it was a breach of trust, that 's all you can make of it. Necessity compelled me to dispose of him. With money in my pocket, what was the use of my coming home ? I took my clothes out of pawn, and was once more a gentleman. Money all gone, I spouted my clothes again, — fell back upon this inexpensive rig, — took to the country, remembered I had a home, and was making for it, when this young man overtook me just now, and gave me a seat in his buggy."

"The matter appears serious," said Lord Betterson. "Am I to understand that you have taken my nephew prisoner ?"

"He can answer that question," said Jack.

"Well, I suppose that is the plain English of it," replied Radcliff. "Come, now, Uncle Lord! this ain't the first scrape you 've got me out of; fix it up with him, can't you ?"

"It is my duty to save the honor of the name; but you are bent on destroying it. Will you please to come into the house with my nephew, and oblige me ?" Betterson said to Jack.

"Certainly, if you wish it," Jack replied. "Get down, Radcliff. Be quiet, Lion! I was never in so hard a place in my life," he said to the boys, as they followed Rad and his uncle into the house. "I never dreamed of his being your cousin!"

"He 's a wild fellow, — nothing very bad about

him, only he 's just full of the Old Harry," said Rufe. " I guess father 'll settle it, somehow."

Meanwhile, Mrs. Betterson had retired to her room, where Vinnie was engaged, with fan and harts-horn, in restoring — not her consciousness, for that she had not lost, but her equanimity.

"Lavinia!" she said brokenly, at intervals, "La-vinia dear! don't think I intended to deceive you. It was, perhaps, too much the ideal Radcliff I de-scribed to you, — the Betterson Radcliff, the better Betterson Radcliff, if I may so speak ; for he is, after all, you know, a — but that is the agony of it ! The name is disgraced forever! Fan me, Lavinia dear ! "

" I don't see how the act of one person should dis-grace anybody else, even of the same name," Vinnie replied.

" But — a Betterson ! " groaned Caroline. " My husband's nephew ! Brought back here like a rep-robate ! The hartshorn, Lavinia dear ! "

Hard as it was freely to forgive her sister for hold-ing up to her so exclusively the " ideal Radcliff" in her conversations, Vinnie continued to apply the fan and hartshorn, with comforting words, until Link came in and said that Jack wished her to be present in the other room.

"Don't leave me, Lavinia dear!" said Caroline, feeling herself utterly helpless without Vinnie's sup-port.

" If we open this door between the rooms, and you

sit near it, while I remain by you,—perhaps that will be the best way," said Vinnie.

The door was opened, showing Jack and Rad and Mr. Betterson seated, and the boys standing by the outer door. Rad was trying hard to keep up his appearance of gay spirits, chucking Chokie under the chin, and winking playfully at Rufe and Wad. But Jack and Lord were serious.

"I have reasons for wanting you to hear this talk, Vinnie," said Jack. "I was just telling Mr. Better-son that you had met his nephew before, and he was quite surprised. It seems to me singular that you never told your friends here of that adventure."

"I suppose I know what you mean," spoke up Caroline. "And I confess that *I* am at fault. Lavinia dear did tell me and the girls of a young man beguil-ing her to a public-house in Chicago, and offering her wine; and Cecie whispered to me that she was sure it must have been Radcliff; but I could n't, I would n't believe a Betterson could be guilty of — Fan me, Lavinia dear!"

Vinnie fanned, and Caroline went on,—

"'T was I who cautioned the children against say-ing anything disparaging of Radcliff's character in Lavinia dear's presence. I had such faith in the stock! and now to think how I have been deluded! The hartshorn, Lavinia dear!"

"Seems to me you make a pile of talk about trifles!" Radcliff said with a sneer. "I owe an apology to this young lady. But she knows I meant

10 *   o

no harm, — only my foolish fun. As for the horse, the owner has got him again ; and so I don't see but it's all right."

"It's all right enough, as far as I am concerned," said Jack. "I won't say a word about the trouble and expense you put me to. But, whether taking my horse as you did was stealing or not, you sold him, you obtained money under false pretences, you swindled an honest man."

"Well, that can't be helped now," said Radcliff, with a scoffing laugh. "A feller is obliged sometimes to do things that may not be exactly on the square."

"I don't know about anybody's being obliged to go off and play the gentleman (if that's what you call it), and have a good time (if there's any good in such a time), at somebody else's expense. I call such conduct simply scoundrelism," said Jack, his strong feeling on the subject breaking forth in plain speech and ringing tones. "And I determined, if I ever caught you, to have you punished."

"O, well! go ahead! put it through! indulge!" said Radcliff, folding his arms, and stretching out his legs with an air of easy and reckless insolence, but suddenly drawing up one of them, as he noticed the tear Lion's teeth had made. "Guess I can stand it if the others can. What do you say, Uncle Lord? Give me up as a bad job, eh?"

"Hem!" Lord coughed, and rubbed his chin with his palm. "If this sort of conduct is to continue, the crisis may as well come now, I suppose, as later; and, unless you give a solemn pledge to alter your course, I shall let it come."

"O, I'll give the solem'est sort of a pledge!" Radcliff replied.

"You will notice — ahem! — a change in our family," Lord went on. "The boys have applied themselves to business, — in plain terms, gone to work. Although I have said little on the subject, I have silently observed, and I am free to confess that I have been gratified. Since our circumstances are what they are, they have done well, — I may add, they have done nobly."

"Fan me, Lavinia dear!" whispered Caroline.

"Hey, boys? what's got into you?" said Radcliff, really astonished.

Lord put up his hand, to prevent the boys from answering, and continued, —

"Your unusually long absence, I am persuaded, has had a wholesome effect. But to the presence of new elements in the family I attribute the better state of things, in a large measure." Lord indicated Lavinia, by a gracious wave of the hand, adding, "Though a man of few words, I am not blind, and I am not ungrateful."

This recognition of her influence, before Jack and the whole family, brought the quick color to Vinnie's cheeks and tears to her eyes. She was surprised by what Lord said, and still more surprised that any words of his could touch her so. He had hitherto treated her with civil, quiet reserve, and she had never been able to divine his secret thought of her. Nor had she cared much, at first, what that might be; but day by day she had learned to know that under all his weaknesses there was something in his character worthy of her esteem.

"If you choose to fall into the new course of things, Radcliff, you will be welcome here, as you always have been. Not otherwise."

And again Jack was reminded of the look and tone with which he had seen Lord Betterson confront Peakslow at the gap of the fence.

"Of course I 'll fall in, head over heels," said Radcliff, with a laugh, and a look at Vinnie, which Jack did not like. "I think I shall fancy the new elements, as you call 'em."

Jack started up, with sparkling eyes; but, on an instant's reflection, bridled his tongue, and settled down again, merely giving Vinnie a swift glance, which seemed to say, "If he has any more of his *fun* with you, I 'll —"

"No more trifling," said Betterson. "If you stay, you will come under the new *régime*. That means, in plain speech — work; we all work."

"Oh!" gasped poor Caroline, and reached out helplessly to her sister. "The hartshorn, Lavinia dear!"

"I 'll stay, and I 'll work, — I 'll do as the rest do," said Radcliff. "But when the Philadelphia partners pony up, of course I have my dividend."

"A word here," said Lord, "is due to our friends. By the Philadelphia partners, my nephew means the relatives who occasionally send us money. Now, as to his dividend: when he came into our family, it was with the understanding that he would be clothed and educated at the expense of those connections. Accordingly, when money has been sent to me, a portion has always gone to him. As soon as he gets money, it burns him till he goes off and squanders it. When it is gone, he comes home here, and waits for another supply."

Then Jack spoke up.

"I say, when the next supply comes, eighty dollars of it — if there's as much — should be paid over to that truckman he swindled. I insist upon that."

Radcliff snapped his fingers. "That's a foolish way of doing business!"

"Foolish or not," cried Jack, "you shall agree to it."

"You have anticipated me," remarked Betterson, with a high courtesy contrasting with Jack's haste and heat. "I was about to propose a similar arrangement. Radcliff's money passes through my hands. I will see to it, — the truckman shall be paid. Do you agree, Radcliff? If not, I have nothing more to urge."

"Of course I agree, since I can't help myself. But next time I have a horse to dispose of," Radcliff added with a derisive smile at Jack, "I shall go farther. So take care!"

"No need of giving me that warning," Jack made answer, rising to his feet. He went over and stood by Vinnie, and looked back with strong distrust upon the jeering Radcliff. "I don't know that I do right, Mr. Betterson; but I'll leave him here, if you say so."

"I think it best, on the whole," Mr. Betterson replied.

"O, bosh!" cried Radcliff, giving Jack a sinister look. "You and I'll be better acquainted, some day! Come, boys, show me what you've been about lately. And, see here, Rufe,—have n't I got a pair of pants about the house somewhere? See how that dog tore my trousers-leg! I'll pay *him* my compliments, too, some time!"

As he was walking out of the house, Lion at the door gave a growl. Jack silenced the dog, and then took leave. Vinnie urged him to stay to supper.

"It will be ready in five minutes," she said; "I was just going to set the table when you came."

But Jack replied, with a bitter smile, that he believed his appetite would be better after a ride of a few miles in the open air.

"Look out for the scamp!" he whispered in her ear; and then, with brief good-byes to the rest, he sprang into the buggy, called Lion to a seat by his side, and drove away.

CHAPTER XXXII.

AN IMPORTANT EVENT.

RADCLIFF resumed his place in the family. But he soon found that his relations to it were no longer what they had been before the days of Vinnie and Jack.

The "new elements" had produced a greater change than he supposed. He no longer possessed the boundless influence over the boys which his wild spirits formerly gave him. They saw him in the light of this last revelation of his character, and contrasted his coarse foolery, once so attractive, with the gentle manners and cheerful earnestness of Vinnie and Jack; in which comparison this flower of the Betterson stock suffered blight.

The boys did not take a holiday in honor of Rad's return, but went steadily on with their tasks. Lord Betterson himself seemed suddenly to have changed his views of things, for he now offered to assist the boys in repairing the fences, for which they had been cutting poles in the woods.

Rad worked a little, but, seeing how things were going, sulked a good deal more. He tried to be very gallant toward Vinnie, but her quiet dignity of manner was proof against all his pleasantries. Even

Cecie and Lill could not somehow enjoy his jests as they used to; and Caroline — there was no disguising the fact — had ceased to view his faults through the golden haze of a sentimental fancy.

So Radcliff found himself out of place, unappreciated; and discontent filled his soul. At length an event occurred which blew his smouldering restlessness into a flame.

The "Philadelphia partners" were heard from.

Rufe and Wad, who had been over to the Mills one day, completing their arrangements with the pump-maker for boring the logs of their aqueduct, brought home from the mail one of those envelopes whose post-mark and superscription always gladdened the eyes of the Bettersons.

It was from Philadelphia, and it contained a draft for two hundred and fifty dollars.

One third of this sum was for Radcliff's "benefit."

It would have been wise, perhaps, to keep from him the knowledge of this fact; but it would have been impossible.

"A pittance, a mere pittance," said Lord, holding the precious bit of paper up to the light. "Uncle George could just as well have made it a thousand, without feeling it. However, small favors gratefully received." And he placed the draft in his pocket-book with calm satisfaction.

Joy overflowed the family; Caroline began to build fresh castles in the air; and Vinnie heard Radcliff say to the boys, —

"You can afford to lay by now, and have a good time, with that money."

"Radcliff Betterson!" cried Vinnie, "you provoke me!"

"How so, my charmer?" said Rad, bowing and smiling saucily.

"With your foolish talk. But I hope — yes, I know — the boys will pay no attention to it. To stop work now, and go and play, just because a little money has come into the house, — I should lose all my respect for them, if they were to do so silly a thing."

"Well, I was only joking," said Rad.

"We could very well spare some of your jokes," Vinnie replied.

"And me too, I suppose you think?"

"You might be more useful to yourself and others than you are; it is easy to see that."

"Well, give me a smile now and then; don't be so cross with a feller," said Rad. "You don't show me very much respect."

"It is n't my fault; I should be glad to show you more."

Such was about the usual amount of satisfaction Radcliff got from his talk with Vinnie. She was always "up to him," as the boys said.

When he walked off, and found them laughing at his discomfiture, he laughed too, with a fresh quid in his cheek, and his head on one side, but with something not altogether happy in his mirth.

"Uncle Lord," said he in the evening, "if you'll put your name to that draft, I'll go over to the Mills in the morning and cash it for you."

"Thank you, Radcliff," said his uncle. "I've some bills to pay, and I may as well go myself."

"Let the bills slide, why don't you, and get some good out of the money?" said Radcliff. "And see here, uncle, — what's the use of paying off that truckman in such a hurry? I want some of that money; it was intended for me, and I ain't going to be cheated out of it."

"As to that," replied Lord, "you entered into a certain agreement, which seemed to me just; and I do not like now to hear you speak of being cheated, — you, of all persons, Radcliff."

"O, well, I suppose you'll do as you like, since you've got the thing into your hands!" And Radcliff walked sulkily out of the house.

The next day Mr. Betterson drove over to the Mills, cashed the draft, made some necessary purchases, paid some bills which had been long outstanding, and called to hand Jack eighty dollars, on Radcliff's account, for the swindled truckman.

Jack was off surveying with Forrest Felton, and was not expected home for a day or two. Mr. Betterson hardly knew what to do in that case, but finally concluded to keep the money, and leave Jack word that he had it for him.

CHAPTER XXXIII.

MRS. WIGGETT'S "NOON-MARK."

JACK returned home, unexpectedly, that night. He jumped for joy when told of Mr. Betterson's call and the message he had left. The promise of money due himself could not have pleased him so much as the prospect now presented of justice being done to the truckman.

He felt some concern, it must be owned, lest the money should, after all, be diverted from its course; he determined, therefore, to act promptly in the matter, and go to Long Woods the next day.

He and Forrest were laying out town lots somewhere up the river; and he was closely occupied all the next forenoon and a part of the afternoon with his calculations and drawings.

At last he leaped up gayly, with that sense of satisfaction and relief which comes from the consciousness of work well done.

He harnessed Snowfoot, put his compass into the buggy, thinking he would give Mrs. Wiggett her noon-mark this time without fail, winked assent at Lion, eager to accompany him, and drove off with a feeling of enjoyment, to which the thought of some one he was going to meet gave a wonderful zest.

As it was getting late in the day when he reached the settlement, he stopped only a moment at the "castle," to speak with Vinnie, and leave word that he would call and see Mr. Betterson on his way back; then drove on to Mr. Wiggett's log-cabin.

His reception there was most cordial, especially when it was found that he had come with his compass, prepared to make the noon-mark.

"House don't front no sort of a way," said the old man; "and I reckon you 'll have to give us a kin' of a slantin'diclar line from 'bout this yer direction," indicating a wood-pile by the road.

The little Wiggetts meanwhile thronged the doorway, staring at Jack and his strange machine, and their old acquaintance, the dog.

"Cl'ar the kitchen, you young uns!" the mother stormed after them, cuffing right and left. "Noonmark 'll cut ye plumb in tew, 'f ye don't scatter! It 's comin' into this yer door, like it was a bullet from pap's rifle!"

The grimy faces and bare legs "scattered"; while Mrs. Wiggett called to Jack, —

"How long 'fore ye gwine to shute that ar thing off? 'Low I oughter scoop up a little fust."

"Scoop up?" Jack repeated, not quite taking her meaning.

"Right smart o' dirt on the floor yer; it 'll be in your way, I reckon."

"Not at all," said Jack. "My line will cut through; and you can *scoop* down to it, at your leisure. I must get you to remove these iron wedges, Mr. Wiggett; the needle won't work with so much iron near."

The wedges removed, the needle settled; and Jack, adjusting the sights of his compass to a north-and-south line, got Mr. Wiggett to mark its bearings for him, with a chalk pencil, on the floor of the open doorway.

"All creation!" shrieked the woman, suddenly making a pounce at the kneeling old man; "we don't want a noon-mark thar, cl'ar away from the jamb, ye fool! We want it whur the shadder o' the jamb 'll hit it plumb at noon."

The old man looked up from his position on "all-fours," and parried her attack with his lifted hand.

"Ye mout wait a minute!" he said; "then you 'll see if me an' this yer youngster 's both fools. I had a lesson that larnt me onct that he knows better 'n I dew what he 's about; an' I 'lowed, this time, I 'd go by faith, an' make the marks 'thout no remarks o' my own."

"The line will come just where you want it, Mrs. Wiggett," Jack assured her, hiding a laugh behind his compass.

Having got the old man to mark two points on his north-and-south line, one at the threshold and the other a little beyond, Jack put his rule to them and drew a pencil-line; Mrs. Wiggett watching with a jealous scowl, not seeing that her mark was coming where she wanted it, — "right ag'in the jamb," — after all.

Then, by a simple operation, which even she understood, Jack surprised her.

He first measured the distance of his line from the jamb. Then he set off two points, on the same side, at the same distance from the line, farther along on the floor. Then through these points he drew a second line, parallel to the first, and touching the corner of the jamb, by which the noon shadow was to be cast. Into this new line Jack sank his noon-mark with a knife.

"There," said he, "is a true noon-mark, which will last as long as your house does,"—a prediction which, by a very astonishing occurrence, was to be proved false that very afternoon.

"I reckon the woman is satisfied," said the old man; "anyhow, I be; an' now what's the tax for this yer little scratch on the floor?"

"Not anything, Mr. Wiggett."

"Hey? ye make noon-marks for folks 'thout pay?"

"That depends. Sometimes, when off surveying, I'm hailed at the door of a house, and asked for a noon-mark. I never refuse it. Then, if convenient, I take my pay by stopping to dinner or supper. But I never accept money."

"Sartin!" cried the old man. "Yer, ol' woman!" (it must be remembered that Mrs. Wiggett was forty years younger than her husband), "fly round,—make things hum,—git up a supper as suddent as ye kin, an' ax our friend yer. Whur's that Sal?"

Mrs. Wiggett, who had appeared all pride and sunny smiles regarding her noon-mark (particularly after hearing it was not to be paid for), fell suddenly into a stormy mood, and once more began to cuff the children right and left.

Jack hastened to relieve her mind by saying that Mr. Wiggett had quite mistaken his meaning; that he had an engagement which must deprive him of the pleasure of taking supper with her and her interesting family. Thereupon she brightened again. The old man shook him warmly by the hand; and Jack, putting his compass into the buggy, drove back up the valley road.

Vinnie had told him that the Betterson boys were cutting logs for their aqueduct; and hearing the sound of an axe on his way back, Jack tied Snowfoot to a sapling by the road, and went up into the woods to find them.

"What! you coming too, Lion?" he said, after he had gone several rods. "Did n't I tell you to watch? Well, I believe I did n't. Never mind; Snowfoot is hitched."

He found Rufe and Wad cutting trees with great industry, having determined to have the logs laid from the spring to the house without delay.

"We've taken the farm of father, as you suggested," said Wad. "He is helping us do the fall ploughing while we get out our logs. He and Link are at it with the oxen, over beyond the house, now."

"And where's that precious cousin of yours?"

"I believe he has gone to the house to see if supper is about ready," said Rufe. "He's smart to work, when he does take hold, but his interest does n't hold out, and the first we know, he is off."

Jack stopped and talked with the boys about their water-works for about half an hour. Then Rad came up through the woods, by way of the spring, and announced that supper was ready, greeting Jack with a jeering laugh.

"You 'll take tea with us, of course," Rufe said to Jack.

"I suppose your father will be at the house by this time; I 'll stop and see him, at any rate," was Jack's reply.

Rufe went with him down through the woods to where Snowfoot was left hitched. As they were getting into the buggy, Rufe noticed Zeph Peakslow coming out of some bushes farther down the road, and going towards home.

"See him slink off?" said Rufe. "He 's afraid of me yet; but he need n't be, — I 've promised Vinnie not to meddle with him."

Then, on the way home, Rufe surprised Jack by telling him how Vinnie had made acquaintance with the Peakslow family, and how Mrs. Peakslow, taking advantage of her husband's absence from home, had called on the Bettersons, under pretence of returning Vinnie's box of salve.

Mr. Betterson had not yet come to the house; and Jack, having hitched Snowfoot to an oak-tree, and told of his business with the Wiggetts, asked Vinnie and her sister if they would not like a noon-mark on their floor. "It will be a good thing to set your clock by when it goes wrong," he explained.

Vinnie gladly accepted the offer.

"And, O Jack!" she said, "I wish you would give Mrs. Peakslow one too."

"I would, certainly," said Jack; "but" (his pride coming up) "would n't it look as if I was anxious to make my peace with Peakslow?"

"Never mind that; I think even he will appreciate the kindness. I wish you would!"

"I will — to please you," said Jack. "This afternoon, if I have time." And he went to the buggy for his compass.

He fumbled in the blanket under the seat, looked before and behind, and uttered an exclamation.

"What 's the trouble, Jack?" Rufe asked.

"It is gone! my compass is gone!" said Jack. "Somebody has taken it."

"That Zeph — we saw him, you know!" said Rufe. "It 's one of his tricks."

"I 'll overhaul that Zeph!" said Jack; "I 'll teach him to play his tricks on me!"

Vinnie ran after him as he was starting off.

"Jack! don't be hasty or unkind!"

"O no! I won't be unkind," said Jack, with something bitter in his laugh. "I just want my compass, that 's all." And he hurried down the road.

CHAPTER XXXIV.

THE STRANGE CLOUD.

JACK'S call on the Peakslows was brief and unsatisfactory. He returned to the "castle" without his compass, and looking flushed and disturbed.

"I did n't accuse Zeph of stealing," said Jack, fearful of being blamed by Vinnie. "They were at supper; and I just said, 'Zeph, my boy, what did you do with my compass?' He denied having touched it. I explained. Great commotion. Mamma Peakslow looked frightened out of her wits, and papa blazed away at me like a seventy-four-gun ship. In short, you will have to wait for your noon-mark, Mrs. Betterson. So will Mrs. Peakslow. I did n't tell her I was going to make her one, if Zeph had n't stolen my compass."

"But you don't know he stole it," said Vinnie.

"We don't know that he and Dud put rubbish in our spring," Rufe made answer for Jack, "and yet we know it as well as we know anything we don't know."

"I can't tell what I was thinking of," said Jack, "to leave any property of mine unguarded, within reach of the Peakslows. Lion was up in the woods with me before I knew it."

"Where are you going now?" Vinnie asked.

"To look for my compass in the bushes. Zeph must have hid it somewhere, for he did n't have it when we saw him."

"Wait till after supper, and I will go with you," said Rufe. "Father is here now."

Mr. Betterson was coming up from the stable, accompanied by Radcliff. Rad had hastened to waylay him, and make a last appeal for the money which he knew Jack was waiting to receive. He talked and gesticulated earnestly; but Lord shook his head and compressed his lips with great firmness, whereupon Rad, instead of coming to supper with the rest, wandered sulkily away.

When Mr. Betterson had washed his hands and face, and brushed his hair, and put on his threadbare black coat and frayed stock, the family sat down at the table. Jack waited unwillingly, and soon excused himself, saying he must look for his compass before dark.

"I 'll attend to our truckman's little matter when I come back," he said, and hurried away.

Link jumped up from the table and went with him; Rufe and Wad promising to follow as soon as they were through with their supper.

Careful search was made all about the roadside bushes where the wagon had been partially concealed when the compass was taken. Lion was also set to hunt. But all in vain. Some faint footprints were found, but Jack could not be sure that they were not either his own or Rufe's.

"Lion don't know what we are looking for; he's after rabbits," said Link. "Was this all the compass you had?"

"The only surveyor's compass; and the worst of it is, 't was a borrowed one. It belongs to Forrest Felton. He has a theodolite which we use for fine work; and I've a little pocket-compass, given me by an old lady a few years ago. I would n't have lost this for twice its value, — it's a most exasperating trick!" Jack muttered. "And now it is suddenly growing dark."

It was very suddenly growing very dark. A strange cloud was blackening the sunset sky. "Did you ever see anything so funny?" said Link.

"It is like the lower half of an immense balloon, the top spreading out," said Jack. "See that long, hanging, pear-shaped end!"

"I wonder if the folks at the house see it!" Link exclaimed, growing excited. "It looks like an elephant's trunk! By sixty, it's growing!"

"It's moving this way," said Jack. "Fast, too! and roaring, — hear it? There's an awful storm coming!"

"Oh!" cried Link, "see the lightning-forks! It will be here in a jiffy."

The "elephant's trunk," which had seemed to be feeling its way up the valley, now swung toward the line of timber; the roar which accompanied it became deafening; and suddenly the cloud, and all the air about it, seemed filled with whirling and flying

objects, like the broken boughs and limbs of trees.
It was like some living monster, vast, supernatural,
rushing through the sky, and tearing and trampling the earth with fury. The mysterious swinging
movement, the uproar, the gloom, the lightnings,
were appalling. And now Lion set up a fearful,
ominous howl.

"A whirlwind!" Jack exclaimed, shrieking to
make himself heard. "I must go to my horse."

"Let's put for the house!" Link yelled.

But hardly had they reached the road when the
storm was upon them.

Shortly after Jack and Link had left the table,
Lord Betterson gave Rufus a small key, and told him
to bring a certain pocket-book from the till of the
family chest in the next room.

"We will have our friend's eighty dollars ready
for him, against his return," Lord said ; and, counting
out the money, he placed it under the pocket-book,
beside his plate.

Rufe and Wad were now ready to go and help
Jack search for his compass ; but a discussion which
had been going on at intervals, ever since the draft
came, was now renewed, and they stopped to take
part in it.

"If I am going to get out to Divine service again,
I *must* have a silk dress," said Caroline. "And, Mr.
Betterson, *you* need a new suit; and you know — we
all know — nothing becomes you but broadcloth, and
the finest broadcloth. What do you think, Lavinia
dear ? "

"I am sure broadcloth is becoming to him," Vinnie replied quietly. "And I should like to see you come out in silk. And Cecie and Lilian need new things. But — how much of the two hundred and fifty dollars is left, Mr. Betterson?"

"Deducting Radcliff's share, one hundred and twenty odd dollars," said Lord, touching the pocket-book by his plate.

"One hundred and twenty dollars will go but a little way, in a family where so many things are absolutely needed!" said Vinnie. "It seems to me I should want to get this room and your room plastered, the first thing, — merely for comfort, in the cold weather that is coming."

"And carpeted, Lavinia dear," simpered Caroline.

"And if the house is ever to be painted," spoke up Rufe, "it must be done soon. It won't be worth painting if it is neglected much longer."

"And we need so many things in the kitchen!" said Lill. "Vinnie knows it, but she won't say anything."

"And lots of things on the farm," said Wad. "If Rufe and I are going to do anything, we must have conveniences. The idea of having such a house as this, and nothing but a miserable log-barn and stable!"

"We can't build a new barn for a hundred and twenty dollars," said Mr. Betterson. "And we can't buy farming tools, and kitchen utensils, and carpets, and silk, and broadcloth, and tea and sugar, and clothing for the children, and paint and plaster the house, all with so limited a sum. The question then arises, just *what* shall we do with the money?"

"O dear! just a little money like that is only an aggravation!" Caroline sighed, discouraged. "And I had hoped some of it would be left for Lavinia dear; she deserves it if anybody does."

"O, never mind me," Vinnie replied. "However, if I might suggest — "

But the family had been so long deciding this question, that Fortune seemed now to take it out of their hands, and decide it for them.

It suddenly grew dark, and an outcry from the boys interrupted Vinnie. The tornado was coming.

All rose, save Cecie, — who remained seated where she had been placed at the table, — and pressed to the door and windows.

The baby wakened in the next room, and began to cry, and Caroline went to take it up. The boys rushed out of the house. Vinnie turned pale and asked, "Where are they? Jack and Link!"

"As well off as they would be here probably," replied Lord Betterson. "Shut doors and windows fast. That horse should have been taken care of."

"Jack would n't let us put him up. I 'll do it now," cried Rufe.

But he had hardly begun to undo the halter, when he saw the utter impossibility of getting the horse to the stable before the storm would be upon them. So, to prevent Snowfoot from breaking away and dashing the buggy to pieces, he determined to leave him tied to the tree, and stand by his head, until the first whirl or rush should have passed. This he attempted to do; and patted and encouraged the snorting, terrified animal, till he was himself flung by the first buffet of the hurricane back against the pillar of the porch, where he clung.

"Oh! what is that?" screamed Lill, watching with Vinnie from the window.

Some huge, unwieldy object had risen and rolled for an instant in the dim air, over Peakslow's house, then disappeared as suddenly.

At the same time Jack and Link appeared, half running, half blown by the tempest up the road. Vinnie watched them from the window, and saw the enormous sloping pillar of dust and leaves, and torn boughs, whirling above their heads, and overwhelming everything in its roaring cloud.

The last she remembered was Jack and Link darting by the corner of the house, and Snowfoot tugging at his halter. Then a strange electric thrill shot through her, the house shook with a great crash, and all was dark.

THE TORNADO COMING. — Page 248.

CHAPTER XXXV.

PEAKSLOW IN A TIGHT PLACE. — CECIE.

THE storm could not have been two minutes in passing. Then it suddenly grew light, the tempest lulled, the heavens cleared, and in not more than ten minutes the sunset sky was smiling again, a sea of tranquil gold, over the western woods.

Fortunately, only the skirt of the storm had swept over Betterson's house, doing no very serious damage.

When Vinnie looked again from the window, she saw Snowfoot, still tied by the halter, standing with drooping head and tail, wet with rain. Jack, hat in hand, his hair wildly tumbled, was already at the horse's head, laughing excitedly, and looking back at Rufe and Link, who were coming to his side. The buggy, he noticed, had been whirled half-way round by the wind, so that the rear end was turned toward the porch.

Through it all, Lill had clung in terror to Vinnie, whose arms were still about her. Cecie sat in her chair by the supper-table, white and speechless from the electric shock which all had felt, and she more sensibly than the rest. Caroline was in the next room with the child, whose cries, for a while drowned

11*

in the terrible uproar, now broke forth again, strenuous and shrill. Mr. Betterson, holding the frightened Chokie, opened the door, and calmly asked the boys if they were hurt.

"We are all right, I guess," cried Rufe. "Wad put for the barn, to make room for the horse and buggy, which I did n't have time to get there. I don't know where Rad is."

Wad now appeared; and at the same time the cattle, started homeward by the storm, came cantering down the woodland road, with the rattling cowbell, and ran for refuge to the barn-yard.

"The big oak behind the house, there, — have you seen it?" cried Wad. "It's twisted off. And where's the well-curb?"

"That flew to pieces, and the boards went up into the air like kites, — I saw them," said Link. "Where's the dog?"

"He's in the bushes, or under a log somewhere," Jack replied. "He was shot at once, with a gun held close to his head, — luckily, there was no lead in it. For a long time he was afraid of a gun; and thunder, or any big noise, frightens him even now."

"Some of our fences look pretty flat, — rails tumbled every which way!" said Rufe. "A good deal of damage must have been done south of us."

"Something looks odd over there toward Peakslow's, — what is it?" cried Link.

"Some of the tree-tops by the road have been lopped off," replied Jack.

"That is n't all," said Lord Betterson. "Sure as fate, something has happened to Peakslow's buildings."

"That is what I saw!" Vinnie exclaimed. "Something turned over in the air like the roof of a house."

"I thought just now I heard cries in that direction," said Jack. "Hark a moment!".

"There comes somebody," said Rufe, as a girl of twelve years, barefoot, bonnetless, wild with fright, came running up the road. "It's 'Lecty Ann!"

Out of breath, almost out of her wits, the girl ran as far as the door-yard fence, then stopped, as if unable or afraid to go farther, caught hold of the pickets, and, putting her pale face between them, gasped out something which nobody could understand.

"What is it? — what's the matter?" cried Jack, advancing toward her.

"House — blowed down — covered up!" was all she could articulate.

"Who is covered up?"

"Don't know — some of the folks — pa, I guess."

Jack did not stop to hear more; but, fired with a generous impulse to aid the unfortunate, whoever they might be, gave one backward look, threw up his hand as a signal, shouted "Help, boys!" ran to a length of fence which the wind had thrown down, bounded over like a deer, and was off.

Vinnie followed; but was soon overtaken by Mr. Betterson and the boys, who passed her, as if running a race. Then she heard screams behind; and there was Chokie, sprawling over the prostrate fence, which he had rashly taken, in his eagerness to keep up with Lill.

By the time Chokie was extricated Mrs. Betterson appeared, babe in arms, tottering out of the door, and hastening, in the excitement of the moment, to learn what dreadful catastrophe had overtaken their neighbors.

"Stay with Arthur and your mother," Vinnie said to Lill; "*I* may do something to help." And away she sped.

'Lecty Ann, met by Mrs. Betterson at the gate, was now able to tell more of her story; and so strange, so tragical it seemed,. that Caroline forgot all about her ill health, the baby in her arms, and Cecie left alone in the house, and brought up the rear of the little procession, — Lill and 'Lecty Ann and Chokie preceding her down the road.

They had not gone far, when Lion came out of the woods, with downcast ears and tail, ashamed of his recent cowardly conduct. And so, accompanied by the dog and the children, — Lill lugging the baby at last, — Caroline approached the scene of the disaster.

The whole force of the tornado seemed to have fallen upon Peakslow's buildings. The stable was unroofed, and the barn had lost a door.

The house had fared still worse: it was — even as 'Lecty Ann had said — almost literally "blowed down."

It had consisted of two parts,—a pretty substantial log-cabin, which dated back to the earliest days of the settlement, and a framed addition, called a lean-to, or "linter." The roof of the old part had been lifted, and tumbled, with some of the upper logs, a mass of ruins, over upon the linter, which had been crushed to the ground by the weight.

Mrs. Peakslow and the girls and younger children were in the log-house at the time ; and, marvellous as it seemed, all had escaped serious injury.

The boys were in the field with their father, and had run a race with the tornado. The tornado beat. Dud was knocked down within a few rods of the house. Zeph was blown up on a stack of hay, and lodged there; the stack itself—and this was one of the curious freaks of the whirlwind—being uninjured, except that it was canted over a little, and ruffled a good deal, as if its feathers had been stroked the wrong way.

Mr. Peakslow was ahead of the boys; and they thought he must have reached the linter.

Zeph, slipping down from his perch in the haystack, as soon as the storm had passed, and seeing the house in ruins, and his mother and sisters struggling to get out, had run screaming for help down the road toward Mr. Wiggett's. Dud remained; and by pushing from without, while the imprisoned family lifted and pulled from within, helped to move a log which had fallen down against the closed door, and so aided the escape from the house.

'Lecty Ann ran to the nearest neighbor's up the river. The rest stayed by the ruins; and there Lord Betterson and Jack — the earliest on the spot — found them, a terrified group, bewildered, bewailing, gazing hopelessly and helplessly at the unroofed cabin and crushed linter, and calling for "Pa."

"Where is your husband, Mrs. Peakslow?" cried Jack.

"O, I don't know where he is, 'thout he 's there!" said the poor woman, with a gesture of despair toward the ruined linter.

"This rubbish must be removed," said Lord Betterson. "If friend Peakslow is under it, he can't be taken out too soon."

And with his own hands he set to work, displaying an energy of will and coolness of judgment which would have astonished Jack, if he had not once before seen something of what was in the man.

Jack and the boys seconded their father; and now Dud came and worked side by side with Wad and Rufe.

A broken part of the roof was knocked to pieces, and the rafters were used for levers and props. The main portion of the roof was next turned over, and got out of the way. Then one by one the logs were removed; all hands, from Lord Betterson down to Link, working like heroes.

Meanwhile, Vinnie did what she could to aid and comfort Mrs. Peakslow; and Caroline and her little company came and looked on.

Mr. Wiggett also arrived, with Zeph, and helped get away the last of the logs.

Under the logs was the crushed shell of the linter; and all looked anxiously, to see what was under that.

A good many things were under it, — pots and kettles, wash-tubs, milk-pans (badly battered), churn and cheese-press, bed and trundle-bed, — but no Peakslow.

It was a disappointment, and yet a relief, not to find him there, after all. But where was he? Dud ran back to the field, to look for him; while the others rested from their labors.

"Did the wind do you much damage, Mr. Wiggett?" Lord inquired.

"Not so much as it mout," replied the old man. "It was mighty suddent. Banged if I knowed what in seven kingdoms was a-gwine to happen. It roared and bellered that orful, I did n't know but the etarnal smash-up had come."

"It must have passed pretty near your house, — I saw it swing that way," said Jack.

"Wal, I reckon you 're right thar, young man. It jest took holt o' my cabin, an' slewed one corner on 't around about five or six inches; an' done no more damage, in partic'lar, fur 's I can diskiver; only, of course, it discomfusticated that ar' noon-mark. I left the ol' woman mournin' over that!"

Jack laughed, and promised to replace the noon-mark.

"There 's Dud a-yelling!" said Link.

The roof of the shed — which must have been the
object Vinnie saw rise and turn in the air — had

PEAKSLOW REAPPEARS.

been taken off very neatly, with the two gable pieces,
whirled over once or more, and then landed gently,
right side up with care, on the edge of the potato-

patch, two or three rods away.   Dud, hunting for his father, passed near it, and heard stifled cries come from under it.   He was yelling, indeed, as Link said.

In a moment a dozen feet rushed to the spot, and a dozen hands laid hold of one side of the roof, under which Jack thrust a lever.   Some lifted on the lever, while some lifted on the edge of the roof itself; and out crawled — bushy head and hooked nose foremost — the shaggy shape of the elder Peakslow.

The roof was let down again as soon as Peakslow's legs were well from under it, and a wondering group — men, boys, women, and children — gathered round to see if he was hurt.

"Wal!" said Peakslow, getting upon his feet, giving his clothes a brush with his broad hand, and staring about him, "this is a mighty perty piece of business!   Did n't none on ye hear me call?"

"Did you call?" said Mrs. Peakslow, trembling with joy and fright.

"Call?" echoed Peakslow, feeling his left shoulder ·with his right hand.   "I believe I b'en callin' there for the last half-hour.   What was ye knockin' that ruf to pieces for?   I could hear ye, an' see ye, an' I wanted to put a stop to 't.   Had n't the wind damaged me enough, but you must pitch in?"

"We thought you were under the ruins," Mr. Betterson replied with dignity.

"Thought I was under the ruins!   What made ye think that?" growled Peakslow.

"I thought so — I told them so," Mrs. Peakslow

Q

explained; while Lord Betterson walked away with calm disgust.

"Ye might 'a' knowed better'n that! Here I was under this ruf all the time. It come over on to me like a great bird, knocked me down with a flop of its wing,—mos' broke my shoulder, I believe; an' when I come to myself, and peeked through a crack, there was a crew knockin' the ruf o' the house to flinders. I was too weak to call very loud, but, if you'd cared much, I should think ye might 'a' heard me. Look a' that house, now! look a' that shed! It's the blastedest luck!"

Jack couldn't help smiling. Peakslow turned upon him furiously.

"You here? So ye think my boy's a thief, do ye?"

"Come, Lion! come, boys!" said Jack, and started to follow Mr. Betterson, without more words.

"Come here and 'cuse my boy o' stealin'!" said Peakslow, turning, and looking all about him, as if he had hardly yet regained his senses. "I had a hat somewheres. Hundred dollars — no, nor two hundred — won't pay the damage done to me this day."

"But the children, they are all safe," said Mrs. Peakslow, "and we ought to be thankful."

"Thankful! Look a' that linter! *Three* hundred won't do it!"

"O pa!" cried Zeph, "you've got a great gash on the back o' your head!"

"Never mind the gash," said Peakslow, putting up

his hand. " That 'll heal itself. Holes in the buildin's won't."

Vinnie meanwhile conferred with Jack and Mr. Betterson, as they were about going away; and also called her sister, and afterward Mrs. Peakslow, to the consultation.

" O, I don't know, Lavinia dear!" said Caroline in great distress of mind.

But Lord Betterson spoke out manfully, —

" Lavinia is right. Mrs. Peakslow, we have plenty of spare room in our house, which you are welcome to till you can do better."

" O Mr. Betterson!" the poor woman sobbed out, quite overcome by this unexpected kindness, "you are too good!"

" I beg your pardon," replied Lord Betterson, in his most gracious manner. " We wish simply to do as we might wish neighbors to do by us under similar circumstances. Our boys will help yours get your things over to my house, — whatever you want, Mrs. Peakslow."

Lord did not much mind the woman's outburst of tears and thanks; but when he observed the look of admiration and gratitude in Vinnie's deep eyes, fixed upon him, he felt an unaccustomed thrill.

Mrs. Peakslow went weeping back to her husband.

" I am sorry you spoke as you did," she said. " We all thought you was under the linter; and they was all workin' so hard — as if they had been our best friends — to get you out."

"Best friends!" repeated Peakslow, with a snort of angry contempt.

"Yes, pa; and now, — will you believe it? — now that we have n't a ruf to our heads, they offer us shelter in *their* house!"

"In the castle? — huh!" sneered Peakslow. "I never thought 't would come to that!"

"Where else *can* we go?" said Mrs. Peakslow. "It's 'most night, — nights are beginnin' to be cold, — and think o' the children! 'T will be weeks, I s'pose, 'fore ye can rebuild."

"If I could n't rebuild in all eternity, I would n't set foot in Lord Betterson's castle!" said Peakslow. He looked again at the ruined house, then at the children, and added: "Me an' the boys, we can stop in the stable, or dig holes in the stack, to make ourselves comf'table. Do what you 're a min' ter, for the rest. But don't say *I* told ye to ask or accept a favor of *them*."

The Bettersons, Vinnie, and Jack were waiting between the ruined house and the road; and Mrs. Betterson was saying, "Lillie, you and I *must* be going back; remember, we left Cecie all alone; and the evening air is too chill for the baby," when Link cried, —

"Who's that coming down the road?"

All turned; and Vinnie and Jack and Link ran out to look. They could scarcely believe their eyes.

"It can't be!" said Vinnie.

"Yes, it is," exclaimed Link; "it's her — it's her!"

"Who?" Caroline inquired anxiously, dreading some new calamity.

"Cecie! Cecie, sure as the world!" said two or three at once.

It was indeed the little invalid, who, though she had scarcely taken a step without help for many months, was actually coming down the road, walking, and walking fast, without even the crutch she had sometimes tried to use!

She was beckoning and calling. Jack and Vinnie and the boys ran to meet her. She was pale and very much excited, and it was some time before she could speak coherently.

"Radcliff!" was almost her first word.

"What about Radcliff? where is he?" Vinnie asked.

"Gone!"

"Gone where?"

"I don't know. He came into the house—he saw the pocket-book and money on the table—I told him he must n't take them!"

"And did he?" said Rufe.

"Yes. He only laughed at me. He said his chance had come."

"Which way did he go?"

"He drove up through the woods."

"Drove?" echoed Jack.

"He took the horse and buggy."

"*My* horse and buggy!" And Jack, followed by Lion and Rufe and Link, started up the road.

Though shocked at Radcliff's conduct, Vinnie thought less of the loss of the money, and of the horse and buggy, than of the seeming miracle in Cecie's case.

"How could you walk so, Cecie?"

"I don't know. I suppose it was the excitement. Strength came to me. I called, but could not make anybody hear, and I thought you ought to know."

Mr. Betterson would have carried her home in his arms, but she would not let him.

"I can walk better and better! That numbness of my limbs is almost gone. I believe I am going to be cured, after all!"

CHAPTER XXXVI.

"ON THE WAR TRAIL."

THERE could be no mistake about it, — pocketbook and money, and horse and buggy, were gone with Radcliff.

"He has taken the road to Chicago," said Jack, easily tracking the wheels after the recent rain. "But he'll find it not so easy selling the horse there a second time."

"But he'll spend all that money," said Rufe. "He'll find it easy enough to do that."

"I wish it was n't night," said Jack. "I would track him! And I will as it is. Have you a lantern?"

"Yes — I'll go with you! Shall we take the mare and one-horse wagon?"

"If you like. But, Rufe, if you go with me, you'll have to travel all night. I am on the war trail!"

"I 'm with you!" said Rufe; and he gave an Indian war-whoop.

Mr. Betterson, coming up, approved of this resolution. "And, boys," he said, "if you *should* lay hands on Radcliff, you may as well bring him back with you. We'll try to have a more satisfactory settlement with him this time."

Jack left his friends to harness the mare to the wagon, and went on alone, with Lion and the lantern, up through the woods.

For a while he had no trouble in following the fresh marks of hoofs and wheels over the wet ground. But when he reached the prairie, an unforeseen difficulty appeared. The rain had not extended so far, and the tracks were not easily distinguished.

It was nearly dark when Rufe, following in the wagon, emerged from the woods. Lonesome and gloomy stretched the great prairie before him, under a sky of flying clouds. The insects of the autumn night filled the air with their shrill, melancholy notes. An owl hooted in the forest; a pair of whippoorwills were vociferating somewhere in the thickets; and far off on the prairie the wolves howled. Now and then a rift of dark blue sky and a few wildly hurrying stars were visible through the flocking clouds. No other light, or sign of life, until Rufe descried far before him in the darkness a waving, ruddy gleam, and knew it was the ray from the lantern swinging in Jack's hand.

Driving on as fast as the mare's somewhat decrepit paces would allow, he found Jack waiting for him at a point where the road divided, one branch taking a northerly direction, the other trending easterly, toward the great road to Chicago.

"Here's a puzzle," said Jack, as Rufe drove up. "I've tracked the fellow as far as here, notwithstanding he has tried the trick of driving off on the prairie in two or three places. But here, instead of taking the direct road to Chicago, as we supposed, he has taken this by-road, if my eyes are good for anything. Lion says I am right; for I believe I've made him understand we are hunting Snowfoot."

Rufe jumped down from the wagon, and saw by the light of the lantern the imperfect and yet peculiar marks of Snowfoot's rather smooth-worn shoes, and of the narrow wheel-tires.

"It is a game of his to mislead us," said Rufe. "I believe if we follow him on to where this by-road crosses the main road, we shall find he has there turned off toward the city."

"Go ahead, Lion; find Snowfoot!" cried Jack, and jumped into the wagon with Rufe.

They got on as fast as they could; but the pursuit was necessarily slow, for not only was the mare a creature of very indifferent speed, but the boys found it useful to stop every now and then and examine the tracks by the light of the lantern.

"The dog is right; and we are right so far, sure!" said Jack, after they had proceeded about half a mile in this way. "*Slow and sure* is our policy. We've all the fall before us, Rufe; and we'll overhaul your pretty cousin, unless something breaks. Now, drive straight on to the main road, and we'll see what we can discover there."

To the surprise of both again, the fugitive, instead of turning cityward, kept the northerly road.

"He is cunning," said Rufe. "He knows Chicago
12

is the first place where one would be apt to look for
him; and, besides, I think he is getting too well
known in Chicago."

"He is bound for Wisconsin," cried Jack. "Whip
along. This road passes through the timber, and
brings us to the river again; we shall soon find settlements, where we can inquire for our game."

"If you can speak Dutch, and if it was n't too late
when Rad passed through," Rufe replied. "There is
a colony of *meinheers* up here; they go to bed a little
after sundown."

As they drove on from the crossing, Jack said,
"That left-hand road goes to North Mills. But I
sha' n't see North Mills to-night, nor for a good many
nights, I 'm afraid."

Jack, however, as we shall see, was mistaken.

The road above the crossing was much more travelled than below; and for a while the boys found it
very difficult to make out Snowfoot's tracks. But
soon again fortune favored them.

"Rain — it has been raining here!" said Jack, examining the road where it entered the skirts of the
timber, "and raining hard! We must be nearing
the path of the whirlwind again."

They passed through a belt of woods, where the
storm had evidently passed but without doing much
damage; for it was a peculiarity of that elephant of
a cloud that it appeared to draw up its destroying
trunk once or twice, and skip over a few miles in its
course, only to swing it down again with greater fury.

The road was now drenched all the way, and the trail they followed was so distinct that the boys did not stop to make inquiries at the log-huts which began to appear before they were well through the woods.

They made comparatively rapid progress up the valley, until they came to a point where the river, in its winding course, was crossed by the road. There, again, the tornado had done a brisk business; the bridge was destroyed, the side of the road gullied, and the river swollen.

Both boys alighted and examined the track.

"Here is where he stopped and hesitated, finding the bridge gone," said Jack. "And see! here are his own tracks, as if he had got out of the buggy and gone ahead to reconnoitre."

"As well he might," Rufe answered. "Look at these tree-tops, and the timbers of the bridge lodged in the middle of the river!"

"He seems to have got through, and I guess we can," said Jack. "I've forded this stream, below the bridge, before now, when I've wanted to water my horse; but it was free from all this sort of rubbish then. There must have been a great fall of rain up here!"

CHAPTER XXXVII.

THE MYSTERY OF A PAIR OF BREECHES.

JACK went out with the lantern upon the ruined abutment of the bridge, and showed a space beside the drift-wood, in the turbid and whirling current, where fording seemed practicable.

Then the boys got into the wagon again, and the mare was driven cautiously forward, by the glimmering light which the lantern shed faintly before and around them. Lion swam ahead, throwing up his muzzle and barking loud, like a faithful pilot showing the safest way. The wheels went in over the hubs; the water came into the bottom of the wagon-box; the flood boiled and plashed and gurgled, and swept away in black, whirling eddies; and Jack said, "This would n't be a very nice place to break down, eh, — would it?"

But they got safely through; and on the farther bank they were pleased to find again the trail of the horse and buggy.

They were now in high spirits. The whirlwind having passed up the river, the road lay aside from its direct path, but still within the area of rain.

"This is gay!" said Jack. "He thinks he has baffled us; and he will put up somewhere for the

FOLLOWING THE WAR TRAIL UNDER DIFFICULTIES. — Page 268.

night; and we won't! We shall circumvent Master Radcliff!"

But soon the boys were again puzzled. Reaching another cross-road, and bringing the lantern to bear upon the trail, they found that, instead of continuing northward, toward Wisconsin, or turning to the right, in the direction of Chicago, it turned at a sharp angle to the left, in the direction of North Mills.

"This move is a perfect mystery to me!" Jack exclaimed. "It seems as if he had thought the thing all over, and finally chosen the very last place one would expect him to make for."

"Are you sure this road leads to North Mills?"

"Perfectly sure; I 've been this way three or four times. But another road branches from it, and passes a mile north of the Mills; he has probably taken that."

But no; after a good deal of trouble — the road appearing once more dry and much trodden — they discovered that the horse and buggy had not taken the branch, but kept the direct route to the Mills!

"It does n't seem possible! there must be some mistake here," said Jack. And every rod of their progress seemed now to increase the boys' doubts.

The road, long before they reached the Mills, became a mere bed of brown dust, in which it required a pretty vivid imagination to distinguish one track from another. The boys' spirits sank accordingly. Lion still led them boldly on; but his guidance could no longer be trusted.

"He 's bound for home now," said Jack, "and he 'll go straight there."

"If Rad *did* come this way," said Rufe, "he was shrewd, after all. He knew that by passing through a busy place like the Mills, he would hide his tracks as he could n't in any other way."

"To find 'em again," Jack replied, rather gloomily, "we shall have to examine every road going out of this place."

It must have been near midnight when they entered the village. The houses were all dark and still; not a ray at a window, not even the bark of a dog, gave sign of life as they passed.

"This looks discouraging," said Jack.

"A needle in a haystack is no comparison," replied Rufe. "The lantern is almost out."

"I can get another at our house," said Jack. "We may as well follow the dog now. What did I tell you? He is going straight home!"

The dog trotted up to the gate before Mr. Lanman's cottage, and the wagon turned up after him.

"What 's that ahead of us?" said Jack, as the mare came to a sudden stop.

"Seems to be a wagon standing," said Rufe, shading his eyes from the lantern and peering into the darkness.

Jack jumped out, ran forward, and gave a shout. The wagon was a buggy, and the horse was Snowfoot, standing before the gate, waiting patiently to be let in.

Quite wild with delight and astonishment, Jack took the lantern and examined horse and vehicle.

"Old Lion! you were right," he exclaimed. "The scamp must have let the horse go, and taken to his heels. And the horse made for home."

"The most he cared for was to get off with the money," said Rufe, not quite so abundantly pleased as his friend. "What's this thing under the seat?"

"The compass!" said Jack, if possible, still more surprised and overjoyed, "which I accused Zeph of stealing!"

Rufe continued rummaging, and, holding the lantern with one hand, lifted up a limp garment with the other.

"What in thunder? A pair of breeches! Rad's breeches! Where can the scamp have gone without his breeches? See what's in the pocket there, Jack."

Jack thrust in his hand, and brought out some loose bank-notes. He thrust in his hand again, and brought out a pocket-book, containing more bank-notes. It was Mr. Betterson's pocket-book, and the notes were the stolen money.

Jack was hastily turning them over — not counting them, he was too much amazed and excited to do that — when the candle in the lantern gave a final flicker and went out, leaving the boys and the mystery of the compass and the money and Rad's pantaloons enveloped in sudden darkness.

CHAPTER XXXVIII.

THE MORNING AFTER.

BRIGHT rose the sun the next morning over the leafy tops of Long Woods, and smiled upon the pleasant valley.

It found many a trace of the previous day's devastation, — trees uprooted or twisted off at their trunks, branches and limbs broken and scattered, fences blown down, and more than one man's buildings unroofed or demolished.

It found Peakslow, accompanied by the two older boys, walking about his private and particular pile of ruins, in a gloomy and bewildered state of mind, as if utterly at a loss to know where the repair of such tremendous damages should begin. And (the sun itself must have been somewhat astonished) it found Mrs. Peakslow and the younger children, five in number, comfortably quartered in Lord Betterson's "castle."

It also had glimpses of Rufe, with light and jolly face, driving home by prairie and grove, alone in the one-horse wagon.

Link ran out to meet him, swinging his cap and shouting for the news.

"Good news!" Rufe shouted back, while still far

up the road. "Tell the folks!" And he held up the pocket-book.

It was good news indeed which he brought; but the mystery at the bottom of it all was a mystery still.

The family gathered around, with intense interest, while he told his story and displayed Rad's pantaloons.

"The eighty dollars, which you had counted out, —you remember, father,— was loose in the pocket. I left that with Jack; he will send it to Chicago to-day. The rest of the money, I believe, is all here in the pocket-book."

"And you 've heard nothing of Radcliff?" said Mr. Betterson.

"Not a word. Jack made me stop with him over night; and I should have come home the way we went, and looked for Rad, if it had n't been so far; we must have driven twelve or fifteen miles in that roundabout chase."

"Some accident must certainly have happened to Radcliff," said Mr. Betterson. And much wonder and many conjectures were expressed by the missing youth's not very unhappy relatives.

"I bet I know!" said Link. "He drove so fast he overtook the tornado, and it twisted him out of his breeches, and hung him up in a tree somewhere!"

An ingenious theory, which did not, however, obtain much credence with the family.

"One thing seems to be proved, and I am very glad,"
12 *   R

said Vinnie. " It was not Zeph who took Jack's compass."

" Rad must have taken that, to spite Jack, and hid it somewhere near the road in the timber, where it would be handy if he ever wanted to make off with it ; that 's what Jack thinks," said Rufe. " Then, as he was driving past the spot, he put it into the buggy again."

" Maybe he intended to set up for a surveyor somewhere," Wad remarked. " He must have taken another pair of trousers with him."

" I am sure he did n't," said Cecie.

" And even if he did," said Rufe, " that would n't account for his leaving the money in the pocket."

The family finally settled down upon a theory which had been first suggested by Jack, — that in fording the river Rad had caught his wheels in the tree-tops or timbers of the ruined bridge, and, to keep his lower garments dry, had taken them off and left them in the buggy, while he waded in to remove the rubbish, when the horse had somehow got away from him, and gone home. It also seemed quite probable that Rad himself had become entangled in drift-wood, and been drowned.

" Feed the mare, boys," said Lord Betterson. " As soon as she is well rested, I 'll drive up to the broken bridge, and see if any discoveries can be made."

Meanwhile, whatever Radcliff's fate, it did not prevent the family from rejoicing over the recovery of the lost money. And now Rufe's attention was called to another happy circumstance, one which promised to be to them a source of deeper and more lasting satisfaction.

Cecie could walk!

Yes, the marvellous effects of the previous day's events were still manifest in the case of the little invalid. Either the tremendous excitement, thrilling and rousing her whole system, or the electric shock which accompained the whirlwind, or the exertions she felt compelled to make when Rad ran off with the money, — or all combined (for the doctors were divided in opinion on the subject), — had overcome the paralysis of her limbs, which a long course of medical treatment had failed to remove.

The family physician, who chanced to come over from the Mills that day, maintained that what he had been doing for the injured spine, the source of Cecie's troubles, had prepared the way for this result; while neighbor Peakslow, when he heard the news, grunted and said he "guessed the gal could 'a' walked all the time if she had only thought she could, or wanted to very much." All which made Cecie smile. She only knew that she was cured, and was too proud and glad to care much what was said of her.

CHAPTER XXXIX.

FOLLOWING UP THE MYSTERY.

In the course of the day Mr. Betterson and Rufe visited the supposed scene of Rad's disaster, and there met by chance Jack and his friend Forrest Felton, who for a similar object had driven up from North Mills.

The river had gone down almost as rapidly as it had risen, and fording it now by daylight was no such difficult matter. But there still were the timbers and tree-tops amidst which the vehicles had passed the night before.

Jack showed marks on one of his wheels where the spokes had been sharply raked, and told how, examining Snowfoot by daylight, he had found muddy splashes on his flank, as if he had been struck there by a bough or branch drenched in turbid water.

" I think," said he, " that as Rad was getting the buggy clear, the limb of a tree turned over and hit the horse. That started him, and away he went. I don't believe Rad is drowned."

Search was made among the rubbish at the bridge, and for some distance down the river; but no traces of Rad were discovered.

"Maybe he has gone home by water," was Rufe's rather too playful way of saying that the drowned body might have floated down stream.

"If he got out alive," said Jack's friend Felton, "he must have found his way to some house near by, in quest of pantaloons." And the party now proceeded to make inquiries at the scattered huts of the Dutch — or rather German — settlers along the edge of the timber.

At the first two doors where they stopped they found only women and children, who could speak no English. But at the next house they saw a girl, who eagerly answered "Yah! yah!" to their questions, and ran and called a man working at the back door.

He was a short, thick-set man, with a big russet beard and serious blue eyes.

"Goot morgin," he said, coming to the road to greet the strangers. "Der been some vind dis vay, — you see some? — vas las' ebening."

The strangers acknowledged that they had experienced some effects of the wind the night before, and repeated their questions regarding Radcliff.

"Young man, — no priches, — yah! yah!" replied Meinheer. "He come 'long here, vas 'pout nine hours, may pe some more."

"A little after nine o'clock last night?" suggested Jack.

"Yah, yah! I vas bed shleepin', somebody knock so loud, I git some candle light, and make de door open, and der vas some young feller, his face sick, his clo'es all so vet but his priches, — his priches vas not vet, for he has no priches, only some shoes."

" Where did he come from ? "

" He say he come from up stream ; he pass de pridge over, and der vas no pridge ; and he dhrive 'cross de vaser, and he cannot dhrive 'cross ; so he git out, only his priches not git out, for de vaser vas vet, and his priches keeps in de vagon, vile he keeps in de vaser ; he make some lift on some logs, and someding make de hoss fright, and de hoss jump and jerk de vagon, and de vagon jerk someding vat jerk him ; and de priches rides off, and he shtop in de vaser, and dhink some, and git sick, and he say de log in his shtomach and so much vaser was pad, and I mus' give him some dhink viskey and some dry priches, and I gives 'em."

" A pair of *your* breeches ? " cried Rufe, eying the baggy proportions of Meinheer's nether garments.

" I have no oder ; I fetch 'em from faderland ; and I gives him some. He stick his legs in, and some of his legs come too much under ; de priches vas some too vide, and some not long genoof. He dhink more viskey, and feel goot, and say he find his team and bring back my priches to-morrow, and it is to-morrow yet, and he not come."

Even the grave uncle of the luckless nephew had to laugh as he thought of the slim legs pursuing their travels in the short but enormous " priches " fetched from fatherland.

"How much were your breeches worth?" Lord said, taking out some money.

"I don't know — I don't keeps priches to sell; may pe vun tollar."

Betterson gave the German a dollar, saying, —

"Allow me to pay for them; for, if I mistake not, you will never see the young man or your breeches again."

He was quite right : the German never did.

Neither — it may as well be said here — did Radcliff's own relatives see him again for many years. What various adventures were his can only be surmised, until one of the "Philadelphia partners," settling up his accounts with the world, left him a legacy of six thousand dollars, when he once more bloomed out as a fine gentleman, and favored his Western friends with a visit.

He ran through his little fortune in a few months, and once more disappeared from view, to turn up again, five or six years later (when Jack and Vinnie saw him for the last time), as a runner for one of the great Chicago hotels.

CHAPTER XL.

PEAKSLOW'S HOUSE-RAISING.

"MERCY on me!" said Caroline, hearing an unusual noise in the front part of the house; "now we are to have the racket of those Peakslow children! What could you have been thinking of, Lavinia dear? I'm sure *I* did n't know what I was saying when I gave *my* consent to their coming. The idea of their turning our library into a kitchen! Not that I blame *you*, Lavinia dear. *I* ought to have considered."

"Surely you would n't have denied the houseless family a shelter?" Vinnie replied. "That would have seemed too bad, with those great chambers unoccupied. As for the *library*," — Vinnie smiled, for the unfurnished room called by that choice name had nothing in it but a fireplace, — "I don't think any harm can happen to that."

Vinnie had a plan regarding the Peakslow children, which she laid before Mrs. Peakslow as soon as the new inmates were fairly settled in the house.

"Since my sister and the baby have been so much better, I have begun a little school, with only two scholars, — Cecie and Lilian. Would n't your children like to join it? I think it would be pleasant."

"Whuther they would or not, I'd like to have 'em," replied Mrs. Peakslow, gratefully. "The chances for schoolin' is dreffle slim in this country; we've no school-house within nigh two mile. But how shall I pay ye?"

"You need n't mind about that."

"Yes, I shall mind too. We must do somethin' for you in return."

"Well, then," said Vinnie, "if you like, you may let one of the girls help a little in my sister's kitchen, to make up for the time I spend with them."

"I'll do it, sartin! You shall have Lyddy. She's a good smart hand at housework, and you may git all out of her you can."

So it was arranged. The little school of two was increased to five; the "parlor" — used only to store grain in hitherto — was turned into a school-room; and Lyddy worked in Mrs. Betterson's kitchen.

"Lavinia dear, you *are* an extraordinary girl!" said Caroline. "It seems the greatest miracle of all to see one of the Peakslows washing *our* dishes!"

No one was better pleased with this arrangement than Jack, who could never be reconciled to seeing Vinnie — with all her health and strength and cheery spirits — doing the hardest of the housework.

Jack took early occasion, on visiting Long Woods, to go and see Mr. Peakslow, and make him a frank apology for having once suspected Zeph of taking his compass. But he got only an ugly scowl and surly grunt for his pains.

For a while Peakslow did not go near his family, quartered in his enemy's house; but slept in the haystack, with Dud and Zeph, and ate the meals his wife cooked and sent to him three times a day.

But soon Dud went to sleep at the "castle," and found he had nothing more formidable to meet than Vinnie's bright eyes, — for Dud had suddenly developed into a bashful youth.

Zeph in a night or two followed his example, and Peakslow was left alone in his haystack.

And the nights were growing chill; and the repair of the buildings went on slowly, carpenters being scarce; and Peakslow, who had a heart for domestic comforts, began to yearn for the presence of his family at mealtime and bedtime.

At length he stole into the house after dark one evening, and stole out again before light the next morning. That did not seem to hurt him; on the contrary, it suited Peakslow; his neighbor's house was better than a haystack. Then he came to supper and stayed to breakfast. Then there was no good reason why he should not come to dinner; and he came accordingly.

Then he stopped after dinner one day to see how Vinnie conducted her little school, and went away looking wonderfully thoughtful. The boys remembered that he did not scold them so sharply that afternoon as he had been wont to do since the tornado disturbed his temper.

One morning, as he was going out, Peakslow saw

Lord Betterson in the yard, and advanced awkwardly toward him, holding his hat in one hand and scratching his head with the other. There was, after all, a vein of diffidence in the rough quartz of the man's character; and somehow, on this occasion, he could n't help showing his neighbor a good deal of respect.

"I 'm a-gun to have a bee this arternoon, — a raisin', — gun to try to git the logs back on to the house, an' the ruf on to the shed, — everything ready, — some o' the neighbors comin' to help, — and if you an' your boys can lend a hand, I 'll do as much for you some time."

"Surely; very glad to serve you, Neighbor Peakslow," Lord Betterson replied, in his magnificently polite way, much as if he had been a monarch dismissing a foreign ambassador.

Jack came over to Long Woods that afternoon, and, having rectified Mrs. Wiggett's noon-mark, stopped at Peakslow's raising on his way back up the valley.

He found a group of men and boys before the house, partaking of some refreshments, — sweetened whiskey and water, passed round in a pail with a tin dipper by Zeph, and "nut-cakes" and "turnovers," served by Mrs. Peakslow and 'Lecty Ann.

The sight of Snowfoot tied to his fence made Peakslow glare; nor was his ruffled spirit smoothed when he saw Jack come forward with a cheery face and a compass in his hand.

Jack greeted the Bettersons, Mr. Wiggett, and

one or two others he knew, and was talking pleasantly with them, when Peakslow pushed the inverted
cut-water of his curved beak through the crowd, and
confronted him.

"So that air 's the compass, is it ? "

"This is the compass, Mr. Peakslow."

"Keep it in yer hand, now'days, do ye ? Don't
trust it in the wagon ? Good idee ! No danger of
its bein' stole, an' your comin' agin to 'cuse my boys
of the theft ! "

Peakslow's ancient wrath rekindled as he spoke ;
his voice trembled and his eyes flamed.

Jack kept his temper admirably, and answered
with a frank and honest face, —

" I have made the best amends I could for that
mistake, by apologizing to you for it, Mr. Peakslow.
I don't keep the compass in my hand because I
am afraid it may be stolen. I have called — as
I promised Mrs. Peakslow the other day that I
would do — to give her a noon-mark on her kitchen
floor."

" How 's this ? — promised her ? — I don't understand that ! " growled Peakslow.

" Yes, pa ! " said Mrs. Peakslow, with a frightened
look. " I seen him to Mis' Betterson's. He 'd made
a noon-mark for Mis' Wiggett, and Mis' Betterson's
sister asked me if I would n't like one, as he was
comin' to make them one some day."

Off went Peakslow's hat, and into his bushy hair
went his fingers again, while he stammered out, —

" But he can't make no noon-mark this arternoon, — we 're all in a mess an' litter, so l"

" Just as well now as any time," said Jack. " The doorway is clear. I sha' n't interfere with anybody."

" What 'll be to pay ? " Peakslow asked.

" O, I don't charge anything for a little job like this, — to one of Mr. Betterson's neighbors."

" That 's jes' so; he did n't charge me nary red," said Mr. Wiggett. " An' he 's done the job for me now tew times, — fust time, the tornado come and put the noon-mark out o' j'int, 'fore ever a noon come round."

Jack adjusted his compass, while the house-raisers looked on, to see how the thing was done, Peakslow appearing as much interested as anybody.

Jack got Link to make the first marks for him on the floor, and laughed, as he looked through the sights of the compass, to hear Mr. Wiggett describe the finding of his section corner, — " runnin' a line plumb to the old stake, out on the open perairie," — and praise the boy-surveyor's skill.

The mark was made with quickness and precision; friends and strangers crowded around Jack with kind words and questions; and he was surprised to find himself all at once a person of importance.

Peakslow puffed hard at his pipe. His face was troubled; and two or three times he pulled the pipe out of his mouth, thrust his knuckles under his hat, and took a step toward the young surveyor. He also cleared his throat. He evidently had a word to say. But the word would not come.

When at last he let Jack go off without offering him even a syllable of thanks, the bystanders smiled, and somebody might have been heard to mutter, " Peakslow all over! Just like his hoggishness ! "

Jack smiled too as he went, for he had shrewdly observed his enemy, and he knew it was not " hoggishness " which kept Peakslow's lips closed, but a feeling which few suspected in that grasping, hard, and violent-tempered man.

Peakslow was abashed !

CHAPTER XLI.

CONCLUSION.

THE house made once more inhabitable, Peakslow's family moved back into it. But this change did not take Lyddy away from the "castle," nor break up Vinnie's school.

The "castle" now underwent some renovation. The long-neglected plastering was done, and the rooms in daily use were made comfortable.

Meanwhile the boys were full of ambition regarding their water-works. The project had cost them a good deal more trouble than they had anticipated at first; but they were amply repaid for all on the day when the water was finally let on, and they saw it actually run from the spout in the back-room! Such a result had seemed to them almost too good ever to come true; and their joy over it was increased tenfold by the doubts and difficulties overcome.

Jack had come over to be present when the water was brought in, and he was almost as happy over it as they.

"No more trouble with the old well!" said Rufe.

"No more lugging water from the grove!" said Wad.

"Or going into the river head-first after it, as you and I did!" said Link.

Vinnie was proud of her nephews, and Caroline and Lord were proud of their sons.

THE WATER QUESTION SETTLED.

"How fine it will be for your dairy, in summer, —this cold, running water!" said Vinnie.

But Chokie seemed best pleased, because he would

no longer be dependent upon precarious rains filling the hogshead, but would have a whole tankful of water — an ocean in the back-room — to sail his shingle boats on.

The boys had also acted on another suggestion of Jack's, and taken the farm to work. This plan also promised to succeed well. The prospect of doing something for themselves, roused energies which might have lain dormant all their lives, if they had been contented to sit still and wait for others to help them.

As Vinnie's school became known, other pupils appeared from up and down the river, and by the first snowfall she had more than a dozen scholars. Among these were Sal Wiggett and two big boys belonging to the paternal Wiggett's "third crap" of children, and Dud and Zeph Peakslow.

The Betterson boys also attended the school, Wad and Link as pupils, and Rufe partly as a pupil and partly as an assistant. Vinnie could teach him penmanship and grammar, but she was glad to turn over to him the classes in arithmetic, for which study he had a natural aptitude.

The Peakslow children, both boys and girls, had a good deal in them that was worth cultivating; and amid the genial associations of the little school they fast outgrew their rude and uncouth ways. It was interesting to see Zeph and Cecie reciting the same lessons side by side, and Rufe showing Dud about the sums that bothered him.

Caroline had very much objected to Vinnie's enlarging her school, and especially to her receiving the big boys. The success of the experiment surprised her. Vinnie had a charming way with the younger children, and a peculiarly subduing influence over the big boys.

"Lavinia dear," said Caroline "what have I always said? You are a most extraordinary girl!"

And now things came round curiously enough; and an event occurred of which nobody could have dreamed when Vinnie set out alone, with a brave heart, to do her simple duty to her sister's family.

It was found that she had a happy faculty for interesting and instructing the young. So when, in the spring, a girls' school was opened at North Mills, she was offered a place in it as assistant teacher, which her friends there — Jack's friends — prevailed on her to accept.

Leaving Long Woods cost her many regrets. But the better order of things was now well established at the "castle" (which was fast ceasing to be a castle, in the popular speech); and she felt that its inmates could spare her very well, — if they would only think so!

Other considerations also consoled her for the change. She would still be where she could see her relatives often; and now Jack's delightful home was to be her own.

THE END.

www.ingramcontent.com/pod-product-compliance
Lightning Source LLC
Chambersburg PA
CBHW060558030726

47498CB00005B/1438